"Gerard, are you still in love with your ex-wife?"

Gerard sighed heavily. "Drop it, Kate. I'm not discussing my former wife with anyone."

"I wasn't a[...] [...]sted angrily, g[...] [...]es or no would [...]

"Feeling th[...] [...], Kate?" Ge[...] [...] taken in her flashing eyes and his tone was taunting. Kate suddenly slapped him.

"Now that you've got that out of your system," he said softly, "perhaps you'd like to kiss me goodbye."

"Kiss you! Why must you be so insufferably arrogant?"

"And why must you poke your nose into areas where it doesn't belong?" he returned icily. But the next moment his arms closed around her, and his voice was hoarse with longing. "Kate, why did we ever have to meet?"

Rosemary Badger, an Australian author, says she always wanted to write, but only started seriously after she took a creative writing course on how to create books specifically for the romance market. Her novels are usually set in Australia, which she knows so well. The author is married and lives with her husband and children in Queensland.

Books by Rosemary Badger

HARLEQUIN ROMANCE

2617—CORPORATE LADY
2629—A GIRL CALLED ANDY
2695—A TIME OF DECEPTION
2749—A MATTER OF MARNIE
2773—SHADOWS OF EDEN

Time to Trust

Rosemary Badger

Harlequin Books

TORONTO • NEW YORK • LONDON
AMSTERDAM • PARIS • SYDNEY • HAMBURG
STOCKHOLM • ATHENS • TOKYO • MILAN

Original hardcover edition published in 1986
by Mills & Boon Limited

ISBN 0-373-02827-X

Harlequin Romance first edition April 1987

For
my sister Terry

CHAPTER ONE

THE child slipped easily over the dunes. Across one bare shoulder was an oversized fishing rod while slung over the other was a pair of giant wading boots. On his head was perched what looked like an old battered fishing hat. He was about four or five years old, deeply tanned and sturdily built. His soft baby hair was the rich black colour of coal and his eyes were as blue as the sky above.

Kate watched him from where she was stretched out on the volcanic rock getting her tan. She pushed her sunglasses back to the top of her head where they immediately became lost in the thick, luxurious mass of copper-coloured curls. A grin spread slowly across her face as she enjoyed the spectacle of the little boy with his cumbersome load. She had seen him before, in fact he was her neighbour, but despite several attempts to talk to the lad, he had chiefly ignored her and Kate suspected he was shy rather than deliberately rude.

Her green-flecked, hazel eyes drifted from the boy to his house. Over the years, small cottages like her grandmother's had all but disappeared at Bargara, the small beach resort only a four-hour drive north from Brisbane on Australia's sub-tropical eastern coast. In their places elaborate brick mansions had been constructed, and the boy's home was the newest and by far the largest.

A tall dark-haired man came out on to the patio and called to the boy. The child turned and reluctantly started to make his way back up the dunes. Kate rolled over on to her back and slipped her sunglasses down again. Ah, the peace of it all, the beautiful peace of Bargara by the sea. How she loved this place! Her job as a reporter at a television studio in Brisbane meant a hectic lifestyle and this was where she came to recharge her batteries.

The rumblings in her tummy reminded her she hadn't had breakfast. She pictured the contents of her small fridge and wondered what she would have. Her demanding job usually meant she rushed meals or did without, but when she was at the beach she made up for it. Perhaps she would have an omelette.

She sat up and adjusted the top of her bright yellow bikini. The little boy had returned to the beach and this time he meant business. He had donned the wading boots, clutching the wide rubber openings under his chin with one hand while he waded into the surf, the fishing rod held tightly in his other. He was going fishing and that was that!

An uneasy prickle crept along Kate's spine.

Her own swim of not more than an hour ago had warned her of a rip tide. Her eyes darted to the boy's house. Surely someone was watching him? Where was the man who had called him back before? she wondered uneasily, as her eyes returned to the child. Incredibly, what struck Kate at that instant was not the fact that the child was in danger but just how utterly alone he looked.

It all happened so fast! One minute he was there, the next minute he was gone. An incoming wave knocked him down, another dragged him out. There was a splash of rubber boots and the hat floated almost peacefully before it was picked up by a wave and tossed out to sea. The fishing rod seemed to stand straight up, the sun catching the reel and sending out a dazzling beacon of light before it, too, was sent hurtling.

The boots had filled with water, pulling the boy under and preventing his escape. The roar of the sea filled Kate's ears as she raced down the beach towards him. A wave picked up the fishing rod one more time, and it was the last thing Kate saw before she dived under and began her frantic gropings for the child.

Kate felt the rip immediately. Its powerful sucking motions grabbed at her legs, her whole body, pulling her out to sea, preventing her from rising to the surface to fill her lungs with air. She held her breath, not fighting the rip but going along with it, knowing the boy was swept up in the same monster. If she was to be any help to either of them she must preserve her strength. When the rip finally released them it would be up to her to swim back to shore with the boy.

But where was he? Her lungs were ready to burst, she felt sure of that. The pain was unbearable and she knew if she wasn't released soon she would be forced to breathe and that would be the end. Suddenly everything became brighter. Her head broke through the surf and she was taking in great gulping breaths of pure sweet air.

The child rose at the same time, his blue eyes filled with terror. Kate reached out to him, touched his small tanned hand, almost had him and then he disappeared. She screamed, her cry gurgling in her throat as she was swept under. She saw his foot and then nothing. Her strength was going and she had swallowed water. Her last thought before blackness started to set in was for the boy. He was too young for this . . . both of them . . . too young to die, and it wasn't right that it should be here at her beautiful, peaceful Bargara. . .

Something gripped her leg, hard, and to her numbed senses Kate thought she surely must have died and was being transported to heaven at an astonishing speed. When her head broke through the swirling foam, she was staring into a pair of incredibly blue eyes set in a face so handsome that she was convinced this was no earthly creature.

He pulled back her head and covered her mouth with his, blowing air into her lungs. She coughed and spluttered, and he held her away just in time for her to empty the sea contents from her stomach. Immediately she apologised in a croaking voice while she wondered how she could have done such a vile thing in front of this stranger.

The boy was there too, slung over the man's broad shoulder, his small face an unnatural white. The man was treading water, one arm under her armpit, and she marvelled at his strength. He pulled her higher out of the water before flipping her on to her back. With her chin tucked snugly in his hand and with the boy crooked in his arm he slowly and laboriously brought them back to safety.

Kate sat hunched in a small ball on the beach watching fearfully as the man worked frantically on the boy. When the child finally moaned, a cry of anguish tore from the man's lips as he gathered him in his arms, rocking him back and forth, crooning to him.

'Matthew . . . son . . . my little Mattie . . . oh, dear God, thank you! It's all right, Mattie, it's all right . . . Daddy's here . . . Daddy's here . . .'

The man hugged the child to his chest, his

eyes closed over the small head, and Kate knew he wasn't even aware of her presence as she sat silently watching. She willed the child to speak, to say something to reassure his father that he was indeed all right. But the child said nothing, and even though he was in the protective enclosure of his father's arms he still seemed incredibly alone. He's like a tiny seedling, Kate found herself thinking, a seedling who has had something vital crushed from him.

When the man opened his eyes Kate saw the fear had gone but the anguish remained. A convulsive tremor swept through his body followed by a ragged sigh as he stood up with his son still cradled in his arms. For the first time he became aware of Kate still huddled on the sand. Anger flared in his eyes and she wondered if it was because she had witnessed his anguish. It had seemed such a personal thing, even to herself. He reached for her hand and pulled her up.

She stood awkwardly in front of him, hoping he wouldn't think it necessary to thank her for her part in the child's rescue. He was well over six feet tall, and the top of her head barely reached his shoulder. His hair was straight and blue-black, the same as the boy's. Brilliant blue eyes were narrowed beneath slashes of jet-black brows, the unusual blue shadowed by incredibly long lashes. There was a deep cleft in the strong square of his jaw and only the full sensual cut of his mouth saved his face from being . . . Kate suddenly shivered . . . harsh.

She dragged her eyes from his face only to be confronted with the broad width of his chest. Through the wet white silk shirt Kate could see the black hairs curling across his chest and working down to a V at his belt buckle. Long, white trousers clung damply to well-muscled thighs. His feet were bare and he was standing with legs slightly apart and Kate felt his stance as well as his attitude was . . . was menacing!

Her appraisal had taken mere seconds, but Kate felt she must be staring. She turned her attention to the boy and raised her hand, intending to stroke the soft hair curving in at the nape of his neck. The man made no perceptible movement, nothing she could ever remember afterwards, but just as she was about to touch the child, her hand suddenly dropped, almost as though the man had slapped or pushed it away! Kate clasped her trembling hands in front of her and the man smiled bitterly.

'You've had your attempt at heroism, Miss . . . ?'

'Chalmers,' Kate supplied quickly. 'Kate Chalmers.'

'. . . and failed miserably!' The man completed his sentence without bothering to acknowledge her name.

Kate squared her small shoulders, while a

warm flush crept across her cheeks. 'Failed miserably, Mr. . . ?'

He shifted the boy higher on his shoulder. 'Hunter,' he lashed out, the bitter smile on his lips telling her he knew she was trying to bait him and how foolish she was even to think of trying. Her flush deepened and spread to the roots of her copper-coloured hair.

'Hunter,' she muttered with a nod. She dragged her eyes from the man's to look at the boy. One little fist was curled under his chin and his eyelids were half closed. Her voice was soft as she said, 'Well, Mr Hunter, if I had a little boy like that I would be grateful for anyone doing what I tried to do and I would certainly never consider telling them afterwards that they had failed miserably. I think I'd get down on my hands and knees and thank them from the bottom of my heart.'

'Yes, I dare say that is what *you* would do, Miss Chalmers,' he snapped angrily, 'but your actions not only placed my son's life in more danger, but your own as well. I saw Matthew go into the water and I saw you race towards him. I shouted for you to stop, but you raced recklessly on, making it necessary to rescue you as well.'

Kate stared mutinously up at him, detesting his smug arrogance. 'I didn't hear you shouting,' she muttered.

'*You* didn't, the rest of Bargara did!'

Green daggers flashed from her eyes. 'Silly of me, I know, but I actually thought you would thank me for at least *trying* to help Matthew, and I was even prepared to say that I didn't expect any thanks, that anyone would have done the same. Now I get the feeling you expect me to . . . to *apologise!*' Her voice was filled with incredulous disbelief.

His voice was filled with unconcealed bitterness. 'My son and I have learned to expect *nothing*, absolutely *nothing*, from your sex! Now, Miss Chalmers, I'm going to take Matthew home and see that he has a warm bath.' Hard blue eyes trailed scathingly over the slender curves of Kate's perfectly formed body, making her skin break out in goose bumps. A sardonic smile twisted the handsome line of his mouth. 'I suggest the same for you!' he drawled.

Kate was left standing with her mouth open as the man, with his small son tucked safely in his arms, strolled purposefully away from her. She watched him climb the dunes with ease, the weight of the boy no apparent burden as his broad shoulders disappeared up the path leading to their home. From where she stood, her own cottage was completely masked by the Hunter mansion. As she walked slowly home she felt troubled and disorientated, her encounter with Mr Hunter and his son filling her with a strange restlessness. There was something odd about the two which aroused feelings of dread rather than curiosity. The man was obviously embittered and it wouldn't take a bright person to realise his bitterness had been brought about by a woman. His wife perhaps?

And what about the boy? He was such a silent little fellow. Children were usually such chatterboxes. Kate thought of her brother's two children and how they could wear you out with their endless prattle. Perhaps the child couldn't speak! If that was the case it could explain the man's manner towards his son. She would never forget the unspoken warning she'd received when she had been about to touch the boy.

Later that same day Kate was in the garden behind the little cottage filling a pan with water and honey for the rosellas which had flocked to the casuarina trees waiting for their treat. The large colourful birds with their bright green, yellow and crimson plumage were squawking in great excitement as their beady little eyes followed her every move. With the pan filled, she sat on the old garden swing and watched them savour their treat.

The garden certainly wasn't what one would call well groomed, she thought with satisfaction. It was a wild profusion of colour and sweet-smelling scents. Jasmine climbed over the pergola, sweeping across to the carport which housed her small Corona. Hibiscus shrubs with their huge blossoms of golds, corals, creams and whites nestled against the dilapidated old grey fence which separated her cottage from the Hunter property. The heady perfume of frangipani blossoms clung heavily in the air, their velvet petals clinging like ballerinas across the gnarled old branches of the trees. There wasn't a thing about this place Kate didn't like, there was nothing she wanted to change.

As she swung slowly back and forth on the garden swing she felt at peace with the world. Not even the thought of her formidable neighbours could disturb this beautiful feeling of euphoria. She leaned back and closed her eyes while the swing rocked her slowly back and forth.

Suddenly her eyes flew open. The horrid Mr Hunter was leaning over her, his face only inches from hers. Shocked, Kate could only stare up at him, completely mesmerised by those hypnotic blue pools.

'You're awake,' he drawled the obvious. 'You looked so peaceful, I thought you must be sleeping.'

Kate jumped off the swing. The man had crept up on her, meaning to scare her, she felt sure. He chuckled softly, the sound like the purr of a jungle cat. He knew he had frightened her and was heartlessly amused. He took her in at a glance.

Her hair was pulled back and held with clips. The small perfect oval of her face was tightened in anger and her hands had become balls of fists held rigidly at her sides. Dressed in a white T-shirt and white shorts she looked like a kid at day camp. He viewed her with amused scorn, unaware of how she was viewing him!

If he had a pitchfork in his hand, she was thinking, he would get the part of the devil in any drama production. In contrast to her white clothing he was entirely in black. A black T-shirt stretched dangerously across taut muscles, and she wondered how he had ever managed to squeeze into those tight-fitting jeans. Earlier his hair had been wet; now she realised it was much thicker than she had thought and it seemed to crackle with a vitality all of its own. She judged him to be in his early thirties and he fairly bristled with life. A dangerous electrical magnetism seemed to radiate from his every pore, making her want to step well back from him but at the same time being drawn irresistibly closer, as though he had the power to rob her of her will. Or so it seemed to Kate as she eyed him warily, wondering how he had entered her own private little world. 'How did you get in here?' she snapped. 'And what do you want?'

One black brow shot up in open disapproval at her tone and she almost laughed aloud at the gesture. She wondered if this little trick of the old raised brow brought Matthew immediately to heel. It certainly didn't intimidate her.

'Two questions,' he drawled. 'Which do you want answered first?'

His soft manner of speaking unnerved her. There was a dangerous quality to the tone. She eyed him through eyes narrowed with suspicion. His manner earlier had left no doubt in her mind that this man would never purposely seek her company. Yet here he was, uninvited and of his own free will. There had to be a reason, and whatever that reason was, Kate knew she would somehow be the one holding the short end of the stick.

'You decide,' she snapped saucily.

Mr Hunter took a deep breath and let it out slowly. It came to Kate he was enjoying this encounter even less than she was. Good, she thought. Neighbours they might be, but friends? Never! Besides, this man probably didn't know the meaning of the word.

'In answer to your first question,' he drawled with exaggerated patience, 'your front door was open and I could see down the hall to the garden. I called out to you, but you obviously didn't hear me above the clatter of the birds.'

The *second* time she hadn't heard him. Goodness gracious!

'There seemed to be no other way to reach you,' he continued wearily, as though bored by this whole awkward business of having to seek her out and having this tiring conversation. 'Both sides of your house are a tangle of weeds and vines.'

'*Shrubs* and vines,' she corrected him. 'Years and years of careful growth created this.'

'Careless neglect would be more like it!' His eyes swept over her garden and he shuddered at what she thought beautiful. Kate bristled at his rudeness but held her tongue. She wasn't going to let him provoke her.

'Anyhow, I haven't come here to discuss your rather remarkable foliage,' he continued drily.

'Why did you come, Mr Hunter? We've already met, so it couldn't be to introduce yourself, and as I haven't had any wild parties it couldn't be to complain about the noise.'

He was watching the rosellas, the birds having earned his attention and not her taunts. 'What are they drinking?' he demanded to know.

'Honey and water, they love it.'

'Obviously.' His eyes returned to her. 'This cottage was deserted until you arrived a few days ago. Are you renting, or do you own it?'

'My grandmother lived here until she died almost five years ago. It belongs to my father now, but I'm the only one who ever uses it. I simply love the place!' and her radiant smile proved she did.

'It's an eyesore!' Hunter observed. 'One good wind and that cottage would disappear.'

'We can't all live in mansions,' Kate replied stiffly. 'I've spent every holiday here for the twenty-six years of my life and I love every rusty nail!'

'I'm surprised your father hasn't considered selling. The land itself is worth a fortune. I should know, I paid handsomely for the property next door.'

'Dad would never sell,' she said, scoffing at the very idea. 'The cottage would only be knocked down and replaced with a hideous brick structure.'

'Like mine, you mean?' he enquired with a sweep of his brows.

'Something like yours,' Kate returned sweetly. Suddenly she laughed and held out one arm. There was a wild flapping of wings as the rosellas fought for position. Several perched on her arm while one landed on her outstretched finger. She offered this to Mr Hunter, but he was in no mood for the sport. Instead of accepting the offered prize he merely glanced impatiently at the gold watch on his wrist. Kate shook her arm and the birds flew down to join the others still at the pan. She sat back down on the swing and gazed expectantly up at him. He returned her openly curious gaze with a brooding darkness.

'I came to see how you were,' he answered

her unspoken question.

Her eyes widened in astonishment. 'You did?'

There was a shrug of broad shoulders and Kate saw this wasn't coming easily to him.

'Yes.' Blue eyes clouded as he met and held her own. 'I might have been a trifle unfair earlier.'

'A trifle, yes,' she agreed quickly, knowing this was as close to an apology she was likely to get but enjoying it all the same. 'I accept your apology, Mr Hunter,' she added generously, thinking she might invite him to stay for a cup of coffee.

Blue eyes glittered with frosty lights. 'Don't mistake me, Miss Chalmers, I'm not apologising, I'm merely implying that I might have overreacted to Matthew's disobedience. He has been warned frequently not to go anywhere near the water without supervision.' Again, there was that mysterious grief in his eyes. He shoved his thumbs into the waistband of his jeans. 'I had a doctor examine him. There's a bit of fluid in his lungs.' His eyes rested briefly on hers. 'Perhaps you should see a doctor yourself.'

'No, it's all right . . . I feel fine,' her voice sounded strained. Mr Hunter was far more worried over his son than he was letting on, and Kate had the distinct impression he was more concerned over Matthew's emotional than physical wellbeing. The man was troubled, deeply troubled, Kate could see that. A picture of Matthew flashed before her as she remembered how utterly alone the boy had looked.

It came as a shock to realise the father was the same. Despite the tall, powerful frame, the arrogance and ruthlessness, Kate knew she was looking at a man who had given everything . . . and lost!

CHAPTER TWO

HE was watching the rosellas, but Kate knew that he didn't really see them. His eyes held a haunted, faraway expression and she wondered if he even remembered he was standing in her garden or that she was sitting in the swing only inches away from him.

'Have the rosellas visited your garden yet, Mr Hunter?' Kate enquired casually, hoping to distract him from his troublesome thoughts.

He swung abruptly towards her. 'What?' He lifted his hand and dragged it roughly through his hair. 'I'm sorry, I didn't mean to sound rude.' A faint smile appeared briefly on his lips. 'Was your question worth repeating?'

Kate chuckled. 'No, but it served its purpose. It brought you back from the pixies.'

'I. . . have a lot on my mind,' he muttered.

'I know,' Kate agreed sympathetically, 'but I'm sure Matthew will be all right.' Her voice was gentle, her concern for the child sincere. Hunter turned towards her. Large hazel eyes gazed up at him, her faultless skin entirely without make-up, adding an appealing softness to her natural beauty.

He nodded. 'He's on medication. The doctor

will check him again tomorrow.'

'Children are remarkable creatures,' Kate said softly, wondering what it could be that was really eating at the man's heart. 'They always seem to bounce straight back.'

The man's eyes blazed down at her. 'Not always, Miss Chalmers, not always.'

'But usually,' Kate said firmly, her hands tightly gripping the ropes of the swing. Matthew's problem, and therefore his father's, ran deeper than the man was letting on. Kate knew she could hardly expect him to confide in her but his hurt seemed so raw that she felt she could feel it in her own heart. 'How about a cup of coffee?' she asked cheerfully, rising to her feet.

'No, thank you, I must be getting back. Matthew was feeling pretty miserable when I left, but I knew he was concerned about you. I think he considers you the true hero in his rescue.'

'Poor little boy,' she sighed, looking up at Mr Hunter, 'I don't think I'll ever forget the terror I saw in his eyes when he first surfaced.'

He held her eyes for a brief tortured second before he turned abruptly away. 'He'll get over it,' he muttered, almost savagely.

'I'm sure he will,' Kate said softly, placing her hand on his arm, 'but sometimes it helps to talk these things through. Matthew had a dreadful experience and he might even suffer a nightmare or two.'

The man glared down at her. 'Are you always so free with your advice, Miss Chalmers?'

Kate's eyes widened. 'Yes, when it's warranted.'

His laugh was bitter, 'Oh, to be so young and yet so wise,' he remarked sarcastically.

'Better that than old and foolish,' she returned evenly, meeting his frosty glare.

Suddenly Kate felt ashamed of herself. She didn't want to antagonise this man, she wanted to help him in whatever way she could. Perhaps she could do this by taking Matthew off his hands for a couple of hours each day. She loved children and would enjoy the company.

'I would like to visit Matthew if that—'

'No!'

Kate blinked. The ferocity of his tone completely startled her. She ran her tongue quickly over her lips, feeling the blood rush to her face.

'Very well,' she managed in a quiet tone. 'I realise he must need plenty of rest.'

'Yes,' he answered, obviously relieved that Kate found nothing unusual in his refusal to allow her to visit his son.

'But when he's feeling better,' Kate continued softly, 'perhaps then I could—'

'Are you hard of hearing, Miss Chalmers?' he snarled, 'Or just plain meddlesome? I don't want you visiting my son. I don't want you anywhere near our place. Is that clear?'

'Perfectly,' Kate said stiffly, thinking she

had never met anyone as rude as the man standing in front of her.

'Good.' He took a last look around the garden, his manner indicating that he found it hard to believe anyone could tolerate such a jungle.

Kate smiled with satisfaction. She was enormously pleased that he didn't like it. When his eyes returned to her, she smiled sweetly and said, 'Plant a few trees, some shrubs and vines and you too can have a garden like this.'

He snorted. 'No, thank you very much.' He raised an inquisitive brow. 'Aren't you afraid of snakes and spiders?'

'Some snakes, some spiders. Why?'

'Because it seems to me you've created a perfect breeding place for both. There must be hundreds of the things creeping and crawling around in that bramble.'

'If I see any I'll give you a shout,' Kate returned flippantly.

His eyes hardened on her face. 'If any escape into my garden I'll call the council.'

Kate laughed. 'The council? Good heavens, Mr Hunter! If you're that terrified of the things you need only call me. I'll lure them back here.'

He wasn't amused. 'My son likes to play in the garden. When he's there I like to think he's safe and I'll go to any lengths to protect him, even if it means getting the council to force you to clear away this rubbish.'

Kate gasped at his threatening tone. On top

of this he was viewing her as if she was a dangerous criminal, or at the very least, a threat to the environment.

'I'll have you know, Mr Hunter,' she said scathingly, 'that in all the years I've been coming here I have not seen a single snake, and the spiders I have seen have been perfectly harmless. Furthermore, I doubt if the council would force me to get rid of my plants. None of them are poisonous, nor do their roots interfere with plumbing or drainage. They'd think you were some kind of nut if you complained to them,' she added heatedly.

He shoved his hands into the pockets of his jeans and scowled down at her. 'You've been warned, Miss Chalmers, I can't do more than that.'

'Oh, yes, you can!' Kate snapped angrily. 'You can mind your own business for a start.'

He straightened and sighed. 'More advice! Very well, I accept. I'll stay on my side of that rickety old fence and you stay on yours—that way we should see precious little of each other. Now, if you'll excuse me, Miss Chalmers, I must go, I've already stayed much longer than I intended.'

'I guess that's what happens when you're having a good time,' Kate said baitingly. But he ignored her taunt, brushing past her to enter the little cottage, his broad shoulders almost touching the sides of the narrow hall as he made his way through to the front door.

Kate followed him half-way down the hall, but stopped when he crossed the small verandah and down the steps to the white sand. He didn't turn round to wave goodbye, but then she didn't expect him to. 'Arrogant fool!' she muttered, her cheeks a fiery red as she fumed quietly.

During Kate's walk on the beach the next morning she came across Matthew's fishing rod which had been washed up and trapped by the huge volcanic rocks. She picked it up and wondered what she should do with it. The rod was obviously an expensive one and she felt it should be returned.

She wondered how she should go about this. Her presence wasn't wanted; Matthew's father had made that abundantly clear, but the fishing rod was like an open invitation. A grin spread slowly across her face. She had found the fishing rod, she knew it belonged to Matthew, therefore it should be returned to him.

But still she hung back. The Hunter home wasn't designed to welcome or encourage visitors. She was only too conscious of the high brick wall facing her own cottage. Also the windows were tinted, which she suspected was for added privacy, rather than to keep out sunlight.

It was well into the afternoon before Kate became impatient with herself and decided that enough was enough, and that she should return the rod post-haste. Earlier in the day she had contemplated making a batch of fudge for Matthew, but decided this would make it seem as though she had planned the visit. Better to make it look spontaneous, something unforeseen. She shrugged out of her pale blue sundress and exchanged it for a pair of shorts and halter top. She picked up the fishing rod, flung it over her shoulder and raced across the beach to the Hunter mansion. Look what I found while I was walking along the beach!

The flagstone steps leading up to the Hunter home were wide and hot under her bare feet. The structure was even more imposing than it appeared from the beach. A magnificent tiled patio stretched the whole width of the house, while gleaming white pillars supported the overhang. Kate stepped on to the cool patio shaded from the hot sun. A massive oak door loomed in front of her, its size and thickness seeming impenetrable. There was a silence so complete that Kate felt surely that no one was at home. She lifted her hand to bang the knocker and wasn't in the least surprised to see that her hand was shaking. The silence seemed to cling heavily in the air and she felt wrapped up in it. Not even the sound of a bird chirping or a bee buzzing. Kate had never known such stillness.

The door swung open so unexpectedly that she gasped. Mr Hunter stood there, his expression far from welcoming, and Kate found herself wondering what it would take to remove the chill which always seemed to be a permanent factor in those deep, almost violet blue eyes. He was immaculately dressed in pale grey slacks and open-necked navy blue silk shirt.

'Miss Chalmers,' he growled in a low voice, his eyes moving from the slightly defiant expression on her face, down to her bare feet planted firmly on his patio. 'I thought you agreed to stay away from here.'

Kate flushed at his rudeness. 'Don't worry,' she said, 'I'm not here to visit, if that's what you think.' She held out the fishing rod. 'I found this on the beach—the waves washed it up. I thought Matthew would like to have it.'

He didn't even glance at the rod she held out to him. Instead his eyes remained focused on hers. 'I guess finding the rod was as good an excuse as any to come over here,' he drawled sarcastically.

Kate's embarrassed flush gave her away. 'I considered a batch of fudge,' she said laughingly, adding quickly, 'for Matthew, of course. Somehow I don't think you're the type to have a sweet tooth!'

His eyes still held hers, causing Kate to feel oddly uncomfortable. 'Oh, and why would you think that, Miss Chalmers?'

Kate wanted to drag her eyes away, but

found she couldn't. It was as if she was being hypnotised by him. 'There's just nothing sweet about you, that's all,' she answered weakly.

A sardonic smile twisted the handsome curve of his mouth. Slowly, he reached for the rod, deliberately covering her hand with his, while his eyes remained fixed on her face.

She gasped, jerking her hand away so quickly that the rod almost fell. Hunter grabbed it and placed it against the wall of the house. His eyes were gleaming when he turned back to her.

'Is there something wrong, Miss Chalmers?' he asked wickedly. 'You don't seem nearly so confident today as you did yesterday.'

'N-No,' Kate stammered, rubbing her hand as she stared down at it. Her eyes swept up to his and 'I . . . I . . .' she swallowed hard. 'Would you please tell Matthew that I was here, and that I hope he's feeling much better?'

'I'll pass on the message,' Mr Hunter agreed. 'Anything else?'

Kate shook her head. 'No, no,' she stammered helplessly, wishing he wouldn't look at her in *that* manner. It was almost as though he was deliberately trying to unnerve her. If this was his aim he was certainly being successful. Kate could hardly believe the effect he was having on her nervous system.

Hunter picked up the rod and examined it. 'It's a pity you wasted your time returning this,' he drawled. 'The reel's missing.' He placed it against the wall and stared at it thoughtfully. 'It's really quite useless.'

'Yes, I noticed the reel was missing,' Kate acknowledged, feeling her strength returning now that he was no longer staring at her, 'but it looked such an expensive fishing rod that I felt the reel could be replaced.'

'Is that what you thought?' he asked softly, once more turning to pin her with those incredible blue eyes.

'Y-yes,' Kate whispered, feeling her knees growing weak again. Damn the man! she thought, as she fought for her usual calm composure. He's deliberately doing this to me, trying to make a fool of me, hypnotising me with his charm and his virility. At these unexpected thoughts, Kate's complexion burned a fiery red. Even her scalp felt as though it was on fire.

'Matthew's fishing days are over, I'm afraid,' Mr Hunter said calmly. 'I'll put this somewhere out of his reach and when he's older, perhaps then I'll give it to him and have the reel replaced.' He smiled charmingly down at Kate. 'You've done your good deed for the day, now be a good girl and run along home.' Leaving nothing to chance, he placed his hands on her shoulders and turned her towards the steps. 'Go!' he commanded roughly.

Kate went, nursing her injured pride. Never

before in her whole life had she suffered such humiliation! At any other time she would have paused and reflected on the almost stunning beauty that stretched in front of her. Golden sands sweeping down to the sparkling blue waters under a cloudless blue sky, while coconut palms rustled gently in the faint sea breezes. Under her feet, purple flowers marched smartly across the dunes, their glossy green leaves vibrant atop the bleached sands.

She turned and looked back at the house, almost expecting to see Mr Hunter watching her from the patio, a gloating, triumphant expression on his handsome face. But the patio was quite deserted and she breathed a sigh of relief. She was about to turn away when something made her look up to an upstairs window. She could plainly see the small figure of a child. Matthew was watching her, his elbows perched on the window-sill, his small chin tucked in his hands. Kate smiled and waved. The child didn't budge, although his solemn blue eyes followed her every inch of the way back to her cottage.

Try as she might, Kate couldn't stop thinking about the intriguing dark stranger and his lonely little son who had suddenly become her neighbours. She was desperate to learn everything there was to know about them, but from whom? Certainly not from Mr Hunter, that was for sure, and she almost smiled at the mere thought. Little Matthew was out of the question. She couldn't very well quiz a small child, even if she did manage to break through the protective wall his father had obviously built around him.

Kate didn't have to wait long. Her source of information arrived unexpectedly that same evening. She was in the kitchen washing up after tea when Mrs Abbott, a woman Kate had known most of her life, appeared on her doorstep. The elderly woman looked tired and worried. Kate was amazed to see her dressed in a white maid's uniform. Kate quickly dried her hands on a tea towel before putting her arms around the woman and giving her a big hug.

'Come in, come in,' she said cheerfully, steering Mrs Abbott to one of the kitchen chairs, 'how lovely to see you! I've been meaning to drive out to the farm, but things have been rather hectic here.'

Mrs Abbott sighed and nodded. 'Yes, I know,' she agreed wearily, 'and that's why I'm here.' She leaned forward in her chair. 'Oh, Kate darling!' she exclaimed, 'how well you look! I've seen you walking along the beach and I've been dying to talk to you, but this is the first chance I've had.'

Kate frowned and sat down at the table. 'You've seen me walking along the beach? But how?'

'I'm working for Mr Hunter.'

'You're *what*?'

'I'm working for Mr Hunter, Mr Gerard Hunter,' Mrs Abbott repeated, smiling at Kate's astonishment.

'But I thought you'd retired. Only last year you said you were too old to do housekeeping any longer. You said you were going to relax and enjoy your farm.'

'I know, but Mr Hunter was so persistent that I couldn't refuse. He came with a letter of introduction from Mr and Mrs Boynton. You remember the Boyntons, don't you, Kate? They were that nice family I worked for for so many years until they moved to Melbourne. It must be five years now.'

Kate couldn't remember, but she nodded anyway, not wanting to distract Mrs Abbott from the much more important subject of Gerard Hunter.

Mrs Abbott continued. 'There was something about the man which made it impossible to say no. I've been working for him for a month now, ever since his house was finished.'

Kate gazed sympathetically at Mrs Abbott, knowing exactly what the older woman meant. Mr Gerard Hunter was no ordinary man. Kate could remember only too well how she thought she had died and gone to heaven the first time she had laid eyes on the man, and although she hadn't experienced any of his charm she had no doubt he could dish it out whenever it suited him, even if it meant cajoling little old ladies into working for him.

'Are you sorry now you took on the job?' Kate murmured sympathetically.

Mrs Abbott appeared surprised. 'Good heavens, no, in fact sometimes I feel guilty accepting the wage he gives me.'

'I don't see why!' Kate protested. 'Looking after a house that size must be hard work.'

'That's just it, Kate, I hardly lift a finger. He has a local girl come in once a week for a thorough cleaning, and the place has every modern convenience you could hope for. Mr Hunter never entertains and I only prepare the meals for him and his little boy.'

Kate smiled. 'But what about Matthew? Surely a child his age is demanding?'

Mrs Abbott shook her head sorrowfully. 'Not *that* child!'

Kate remembered Matthew's unusual silence, his apparent loneliness, and his father's adamant refusal to allow her to visit. 'Is there something wrong with Matthew?' she asked quietly.

Mrs Abbott sighed. 'I don't know,' she admitted. 'He seems healthy enough, but——' Mrs Abbott hesitated before continuing quietly, 'Would you believe that in the month I've been there I've not heard the child speak. Not one single word!'

Kate could believe it all right, she had

already suspected as much. 'Has Mr Hunter offered any explanation?'

'None whatsoever. Actually, it's very sad, Kate, I've seen that man trying to coax the child to speak so many times, but the boy only turns away. It's heartbreaking to watch.'

Kate's heart filled with despair at Mrs Abbott's words. No wonder Gerard Hunter behaved the way he did! He was obviously deeply concerned. 'It sounds as if Matthew needs professional help. Gerard Hunter seems like an intelligent man, surely he's taken the child to a specialist?'

Mrs Abbott leaned back in her chair and sighed. 'I wouldn't know,' she said, 'it's not my place to question him, although he's taken Matthew to Brisbane twice since I've been there. Perhaps they see a doctor then.'

'I wonder,' Kate muttered, propping her chin in one hand, while beating out an impatient tattoo on the table with her other. 'Gerard Hunter is both proud and arrogant, a deadly combination. Perhaps he refuses to believe there's something wrong with his son.'

'Oh, Kate!'

Kate smiled at Mrs Abbott's shocked expression. 'Oh, I know what I'm talking about,' she said, 'I've had a few run-ins with Mr Gerard Hunter already, and each time he's left me with a feeling of helpless rage.' She leaned back in her chair, clasping her hands at the back of her head. 'He must have had a wife.' She peered sharply at Mrs Abbott. 'Has he ever mentioned her?'

The old lady smiled and shook her head. 'You're impossible, Kate,' she said fondly, and then at the expression on Kate's face added on a more serious note, 'no, but I think it's safe to assume they're divorced.'

'Or maybe something tragic happened to her,' Kate mused slowly. 'That could explain why they're both so . . . so *tragic* themselves!'

'Kate!'

Kate had the grace to look ashamed. 'I'm sorry, Mrs Abbott, but something has obviously happened to them, and I am a reporter after all. I didn't mean to sound morbid, I'm just concerned.'

'And I'm concerned about you,' Mrs Abbott said quietly, 'and that's why I've come here. Stay away from Gerard Hunter and his son, Kate. He doesn't want you around. In fact, he told me that if that little hothead from next door comes around I'm to send her packing.'

'Oh, he did, did he?' Kate said, greatly amused. 'So he thinks I'm a little hothead, eh? I must admit he does bring out the worst in me, but better a hothead than a pighead, I always say.'

'Oh, Kate!' sighed Mrs Abbott, 'You'll never change. Anyway, I've performed my duty, I only hope you'll take my advice and stay away from them. Now tell me, how are your parents enjoying Western Australia?'

'Loving every minute. Did I tell you my brother and his family have gone over to join them? He hopes to help Dad with his new business, an ice-cream parlour. Can you imagine it? And Sue's expecting again, after two boys they're hoping for a girl . . .'

While Kate talked her mind was next door, her thoughts centring on the tall, dark-haired man and his solemn little son. By the time Mrs Abbott left, the beginning of a plan had started taking shape in her mind. She arose early the next morning, slipped into her bright yellow bikini, grabbed her sunglasses and beach towel and walked deliberately up to the Hunter home. Her hand didn't tremble when she lifted the brass knocker, letting it down with a huge bang.

The door swung slowly open and Kate found herself staring into Gerard Hunter's incredible blue eyes. He was dressed casually in a pair of white shorts and dark red V-necked T-shirt, the colours and the clothing enhancing his rugged male physique. The sight of him took Kate's breath away and she had to swallow hard before she could speak.

'Good morning, Mr Hunter,' she said politely. 'Beautiful day, isn't it?'

'Indeed it is, Miss Chalmers,' he returned in mock politeness matching her tone, his eyes trailing deliberately across her slender body clad in its very brief bikini. 'But you seem to have lost your way. The ocean happens to be down there, not up here.'

Kate's body was burning where his eyes had deliberately seared it. She felt the urge to run but steadfastly held her ground. She couldn't let her whole vacation slip by without at least trying to help this man no matter how hard he tried to dissuade her. Therefore she ignored his sarcasm and his boldness and squared her small shoulders.

'It's because it's such a beautiful day that I'm here,' she said in a voice so quietly determined that she surprised even herself. 'I would like to take Matthew for a swim,' she continued bravely despite the angry glare appearing in Gerard's eyes. 'I promise to keep a very close eye on him.'

'And why would a pretty young girl want to waste her time with my son? Surely you're up to swimming with the big boys now?'

An angry flush stained Kate's cheeks. 'I thought Matthew might enjoy some fresh air and some exercise.' Somehow she managed to reply calmly.

To her astonishment he slammed the door behind him, grabbed her arm and pulled her down the steps. Kate wrenched her arm free, feeling both pain and humiliation at this unexpected treatment.

'How dare you!' she gasped, rubbing her

arm. She dropped her towel in the scuffle and Gerard bent down and retrieved it, holding the ends in either hand.

'I understand Mrs Abbott paid you a visit last evening,' he said in ominously low tones.

Kate stared at him, her beautiful hazel eyes large in her face. She hadn't thought Mrs Abbott would tell him about her visit, that she would somehow prefer to keep it secret. 'Did she tell you that?' she asked cautiously.

'She did.'

Kate moistened her lips. 'Mrs Abbott is a . . . is a wonderful person,' she blurted out.

'She is indeed.'

'She loves children.'

'I wouldn't have her working for me if she didn't.' There was a flash of white teeth as he smiled. 'She likes you, too, in fact she used almost the same words to describe you as you've just done to describe her.'

Kate was feeling grossly uncomfortable and her cheeks felt as if they were on fire. 'Really?' She chuckled faintly. 'I guess it might be because we've known each other for so long, practically my whole life.'

'Mmmm.' He draped the towel loosely around Kate's neck while he kept hold of the ends. 'Mrs Abbott also tells me you're a reporter at a television studio in Brisbane.'

Kate's face was lifted to his, hazel eyes locked to blue. It was impossible for her to free herself even if she had wanted to. She felt hard muscular thighs pressing against her legs and suddenly her breath was coming in short irregular puffs. Her arms felt like blocks of wood as she lifted them, her fingers like matchsticks as she weakly tugged at his hands holding the towel.

He drew her closer, the backs of his hands rough against the tender skin of her chin, the cruelty in his eyes deepening as he steadfastly held her gaze. Suddenly he released her.

'Well, is that true?' he barked impatiently. 'Are you a news reporter?'

Kate's heart was thumping madly in her chest. She felt shaken to the core. She didn't trust herself to speak and could only nod her answer.

'Well, Miss Chalmers,' he drawled, 'there's no story here, if that's what you're after.' He crooked a long finger under her chin. 'I want to be left alone, do you understand?'

Kate hated herself for being so timid, but under the force of his probing gaze she was helpless to be anything else. His single finger was enough to hold her, and once again she nodded in mute obedience.

'And I don't want you finding any more excuses to come here, is that clear?'

'Y-yes,' she said faintly.

Firmly he turned her round, pointing her in the direction of the cottage. 'Now, go home!'

Kate was only too happy to escape. She

forced herself to walk slowly until she heard him enter the house and slam the door behind him, then she ran. Gerard Hunter had managed to humiliate her thoroughly and completely. She would *never* forgive him!

And she wasn't pleased with herself either. She had behaved like a fool, like a gawky adolescent. It made her cringe when she remembered how she had practically swooned when he held her prisoner with her own towel. What a beast he was, what a horridly handsome, devastatingly cruel beast! Well, she had received the message all right. Wild horses wouldn't be able to drag her near his place again.

She felt hot and miserable as she trudged slowly to the little cottage trying to ignore the imposing structure of the Hunter mansion. It wasn't going to be easy pretending Gerard Hunter didn't live right next door and it would be hard to forget little Matthew.

Her lounge was dark after the sunny brilliance of the outdoors. Kate blinked to adjust her eyes to the sudden change. She almost didn't see Matthew curled up in her favourite chair, sound asleep, his small rosy cheeks damp with tears.

She stared down at him, her eyes widening in delight and horror, a curious mixture.

'My, my, my,' she whispered softly, 'I bet your daddy doesn't know you're here.'

CHAPTER THREE

KATE stared down in wonder at Matthew curled up and sound asleep in her chair. His father would no doubt be worried, if he had missed him. Yet she hesitated to wake him. He looked so sweet with his tousled hair falling over his baby brow, his little cheek pressed against his hands. His long lashes were damp and she wondered what had made him cry. There was no need to cover him. The room was pleasantly warm and his striped navy-blue and white T-shirt, white shorts and brown leather sandals were enough to keep him warm.

Kate tiptoed softly from the lounge. She had a quick shower and slipped into a pair of beige shorts topped with a white shirt gaily sprinkled with chocolate brown bulrushes. Barely ten minutes had passed before she was back in the lounge but, even so, Matthew had gone.

She almost fainted with relief when she found him off the kitchen standing under the shade of the pergola. Troubled, he might have wandered off and become lost.

'Hallo, Matthew,' she said softly, going over to stand beside him. He glanced up at her, rewarding her with a small smile, before turning away to watch a huge cat lumbering towards them.

'That's old Mr Kit-Kat and I see he's right on time as usual,' Kate chuckled, glancing at her watch. 'Come on, Matthew, you can help me get old Mr Kit-Kat his mid-morning snack.' Matthew obediently followed her into the kitchen and watched as she filled a bowl with cat food and another with milk.

'You take this and put it outside under the pergola,' said Kate, passing Matthew the bowl of food. 'I'll take the milk and then we can sit down and watch old Mr Kit-Kat gobble down his elevenses.'

Matthew took the bowl and carried it out to the pergola, setting it down with great care while Kate placed the milk, just as carefully, beside it. The huge cat sat just outside the pergola watching this operation with smug approval. He waited until Kate and Matthew were seated on the old cane settee before he got up, stretched and padded softly over to his fare.

'No one owns old Mr Kit-Kat,' Kate quietly confided to Matthew. 'I think he fancies himself far too clever to put up with just anyone.' Matthew rewarded her with another small smile and greatly encouraged, Kate continued, 'He has breakfast at the Turners' because Mr Turner is a fisherman and there's always plenty of fish. Then he likes to come here for his elevenses because I happen to have the particular brand of cat food he prefers.' She gave Matthew a knowing look. 'He's tried all the others, you see.' Matthew's eyes widened in delight, obviously pleased to be gaining this insight into the habits of the old tom. 'He has lunch with Mrs Tibbitts, who really looks forward to his company ever since her husband passed away. Afternoon tea is with the Swansons where he enjoys a scone or two, and then it's on to the Robinsons' for dinner where he gets all the leftovers from the Robinsons' five children.'

Mr Kit-Kat finished his snack and sat in the sun giving himself a thorough wash. Kate and Matthew watched, Matthew every bit as fascinated as Kate always was at this grand spectacle. She turned to Matthew, 'Should we brush his coat, help him a bit?'

Matthew nodded his head excitedly.

'All right, then. You stay here and keep an eye on him while I get his brush. It's just in here under the sink,' and she ducked into the kitchen to retrieve it. Kate held the old tom while Matthew passed the brush through his luxuriously thick and impossibly long pure black coat.

'Your hair is the same colour as Mr Kit-Kat's,' Kate observed, when the cat's grooming had reached a successful conclusion. 'Only yours is slightly shorter than his, thank goodness.'

Matthew giggled, obviously thrilled by the comparison, while Kate tousled his baby-fine hair, her eyes shining down at his happy little face.

Matthew visited Kate each day after that, arriving in time to help prepare Mr Kit-Kat's morning snack. Together they would sit and watch the old tom bolt his food and then the grooming session would begin. Mr Kit-Kat had never looked so grand! Matthew would leave when the cat did, and although Matthew never spoke to her, Kate sensed the tension easing in his sturdy little body. Whatever his troubles, she was certain they were becoming less and less.

On the fifth day Mr Kit-Kat arrived late, which meant Matthew was at Kate's longer than usual. They had just finished grooming the old tom when a dark shadow passed over them, causing them to look up quickly. Kate could feel Matthew's small body stiffen beside hers, and at the sight of Gerard Hunter her own body went rigid. They gaped up at the tall man while he looked from one to the other, his expression grim, his eyes blazing with anger.

'Run along home, Matthew,' Gerard said quietly, and Kate had to admire his remarkable control although she had no doubt she would receive the full brunt of his fury after Matthew had safely departed. Matthew got up slowly and looked uncertainly at Kate. His large blue eyes were filled with sympathy. He seemed to know what Kate was in for.

She smiled bravely. 'It's all right, Matthew. You go home now and perhaps we'll see each other later.'

This brief exchange between Kate and his son added fuel to fire and Kate knew Gerard Hunter's anger had now reached fever pitch. After Matthew had raced across her garden, ducking through a small hole in the old wooden fence to disappear into his own garden, she had to bite her tongue to keep herself from calling him back. She had no desire to be left alone with his father.

But instead of strangling her, Gerard Hunter walked deliberately over to the fence, examining the hole Matthew had scampered through. Kate cautiously followed, watching in silence as Gerard pulled out rotten sections of the old picket fence.

'I'll replace this,' he said, more to himself than for the benefit of Kate's ears.

'Oh, don't worry about it,' she answered brightly. 'The only reason I keep it is because it supports my creepers.'

He turned slowly to face her. 'Do you think I give a damn about your creepers? It's Matthew I'm thinking of. If he got through here once he'll try it again.'

A lesser person would have shrunk from the

look of contempt on his face, but not Kate. An angry flush crept across her smooth cheeks. 'So what? It's easier for him to get through here than by the beach, and it's certainly a lot safer than the road. Besides, this isn't the first time he's been here,' she declared almost triumphantly. 'Matthew's been visiting me every day for almost a week!'

He had been squatting by the low picket fence but now rose to his full height, towering above her small frame. 'I thought I made myself perfectly clear,' he said, his tone deadly. 'I don't want Matthew here any more than I want you at our place. My son and I want to be left alone.'

'*You* might want to be left alone, but your son certainly doesn't. He comes here of his own free will and he enjoys every second of his visits—in fact, he loves them!'

'I think I know what is best for my son, Miss Chalmers,' he said frostily. 'Matthew wouldn't come round unless you enticed him somehow.'

This was really too much for Kate. 'For goodness' sake!' she snapped angrily. 'I certainly don't lure Matthew here. The first time he came I found him asleep in my lounge when I got back from your place.'

She was about to mention that Matthew had been crying, but something about Gerard Hunter's expression decided her against it. For the briefest of seconds a deep sort of sadness had crept into his eyes, clouding them. The proud, broad shoulders stooped just a little, but the movement and the look were so brief that Kate began to wonder if she hadn't imagined them. His next words convinced her that she had. The man was hard, heartless.

'Well, don't expect him another time.' He looked from Kate to the fence. 'I'll have a six-foot fence erected.' His eyes swung back to her astonished face. 'That should be enough to keep him in and you out!'

'*A six-foot fence!*'

'That's what I said,' he drawled, obviously satisfied with his decision. 'But don't worry, I won't be expecting you to help towards the cost. I'll take care of it myself.'

'Indeed you won't!' snapped Kate, placing her hands on her hips and jutting out her chin. 'There will be no six-foot fence put up here!'

He smiled down at her. 'I wasn't asking your permission, Miss Chalmers. There will be a fence, a proper fence, whether you like it or not.'

'I know my rights,' she told him. 'You can't put up a fence without your neighbour's permission.'

His smile deepened. 'Can't I?' he growled. 'Watch me!'

He turned and hopped over the low picket fence. His eyes roamed across her garden before settling on her hot, flushed little face. 'I can't say I'll miss this jungle.'

Kate placed her hands on the fence and leaned over it, giving him the full benefit of her glare. 'You're a mean, spiteful man!' she shouted angrily. 'That monstrosity you call a house blocks out half my view and all the breezes. I can hardly sleep at night. A six-foot fence will trap the heat in both our gardens. The plants will die. You don't need a fence!'

'What *I* need, Miss Chalmers, is not for you to decide.'

Fearful he would disappear into his house before this matter was resolved, Kate decided a more gentle approach was necessary. With great difficulty she forced a smile.

'Please, Mr Hunter,' she said softly, 'we're neighbours. Can't we at least try to see eye to eye on things?' She had his full attention now and a thrill of excitement shot down her spine. Perhaps she would get the best of him yet. 'Mrs Abbott has already vouched for me. You said so yourself that she thought I was a marvellous person and——'

'Wonderful.'

Kate blinked. 'What?'

'Mrs Abbott said you were wonderful, not marvellous.'

Kate's cheeks flamed with fresh colour.

'Kind of you to correct me,' she murmured, hating the look of smug arrogance on his handsome face. She took a deep breath, letting it out slowly. 'I love children,' she continued. 'My brother has two little boys and since they moved to Western Australia, I really miss their company.' She was earnest now. 'Matthew would be quite safe with me. I would never let him come to any harm.'

He looked at her thoughtfully for a long moment and Kate held her breath, knowing he was making a decision, not only about the fence but his son as well.

'Have you made any plans for tonight?' he surprised her by asking.

'Tonight?' Kate shook her head. 'Why, no, I——'

'Then perhaps you'd like to come over for a drink? Would eight o' clock suit?'

Kate was dumbfounded. 'You're inviting me over to your place?'

A sardonic smile twisted the handsome line of his mouth. 'Come now, Miss Chalmers. Surely a beautiful girl such as yourself is well used to such invitations?'

'Well, yes—I mean . . . no,' Kate bit her tongue. She was stammering like an awkward schoolgirl. 'It's just that I never expected such an invitation from *you*, Mr Hunter.' Her smile was gracious. 'I can't begin to tell you how much pleasure it gives me to accept!'

His own smile was challenging. 'Eight o'clock, then?'

She nodded. 'Eight o'clock.'

'And let's cut the formality, shall we? Call me Gerard.'

'I'm Kate.'

Kate felt she had won a major victory. Tonight she would charm the pants off Mr Gerard Hunter and by the end of the evening they would be great friends. Hadn't she managed to receive an invitation for drinks when only minutes earlier he had told her never to come to his home again? Ah, Kate, you're a wonder woman, she told herself with great relish.

She picked up Mr Kit-Kat's dishes and placed them in the sink. There was no need to check her wardrobe because she knew she hadn't brought anything suitable. Her holidays at Bargara were simple and pleasant, swimming and beachcombing being her major entertainments. After her hectic lifestyle in Brisbane with a job that kept her hopping from morning until night it was peace she was after, not dining and dancing until the wee hours of the morning. Therefore her wardrobe consisted of bikinis, shorts and tops, one or two dresses suitable for shopping, a pair of cotton slacks, a track suit and one pair of stretch denim jeans. Ten minutes later she was in her Corona and backing it out of the driveway on her way to Bundaberg to shop for a dress.

The short drive into town was pleasant, the winding road through Bargara giving her glimpses of the ocean as she passed by the golf course and the various holiday units before she was in the midst of swaying green sugar cane, the cane fields giving the area its name, Sugar Coast.

Bundaberg was a pretty country town, the pace slow and leisurely with plenty of tree-lined streets. Kate parked her car under a giant fig tree and stepped into a smart-looking boutique. An hour later she stepped out again carrying a flat white box under her arm. Feeling enormously pleased with her purchase, she decided she would get something for Matthew as well. A teddy bear caught her eye in one of the toy shops and minutes later she had added another bundle to her arms before heading back to the beach. The rest of the day was spent in getting ready.

She fixed herself a small salad for her evening meal, and ate it on the front veranda facing the ocean while she watched the tide come in. The tides were getting bigger each day and by Christmas the king tides would be in. She wondered if Gerard would teach his son to use a surfboard. Kate grinned to herself. She wondered about them a lot.

'It's the reporter in me' she said aloud. 'I can't help wondering where they're from and why they're here.' I guess they must be from Melbourne, she continued, thinking silently. Mrs Abbott had said the letter he had handed her was from people living in Melbourne. Her fine brows drew together in a frown. But why here? How did Gerard Hunter ever find this beautiful but relatively unknown beach? Had this place been recommended to him by . . . what were their names? The Boyntons? Perhaps they had described it in glowing terms and Gerard had decided it would be the ideal place to bring up his son. She would find out all about him tonight over drinks.

Kate was in the garden feeding the rosellas when Mrs Abbott's ancient Fiat pulled up at the edge of the driveway. She looked tired, her face drawn into wrinkles Kate hadn't noticed before.

'I won't be stopping,' Mrs Abbott said, as Kate started to open the car door for her. 'It's been a day,' she added tiredly. 'First Matthew running off and then Mr Hunter informing me he'd invited you to his home.' She peered anxiously at Kate. 'I hope you know what you're doing.'

Kate's eyes were filled with sympathy for her friend. 'He only invited me to be neighbourly. He wanted to put up a fence to keep Matthew in and we're going to discuss it.' Kate didn't add that the fence was also to keep her out.

'Well, I don't know what kind of an evening you're in for. Matthew has been impossible, and Mr Hunter has been locked in his office all afternoon.'

'Poor Abbey,' Kate sighed, using her child-hood name for the woman, 'you do look tired.'

Mrs Abbott smiled and brightened. 'I'll be fine after a good night's sleep.' She adjusted the gears of the car. 'Well, I'm off. Take care tonight. I'm not so old that I can't remember what it's like to be with a good-looking man like Mr Hunter.' She gave Kate a knowing wink. 'And don't think you can fool me by saying your interest is strictly professional!'

Kate laughed goodnaturedly as the old Fiat carried Mrs Abbott down the road to her small farm a few kilometres away, staying to wave until the car was out of sight.

She dressed with care for the evening, starting her preparations with a leisurely bath sprinkled with sweet-smelling bath salts and ended by standing in front of her bedroom mirror surveying the final results. The dress was more than she had hoped for, of a creamy white silk which clung to her slender curves in a daringly provocative manner. The neckline was just low enough to offer a tantalising glimpse of cleavage, the soft swell of her breasts rising and falling against the feather-soft material. A touch of expertly applied make-up added drama and depth to her beautiful hazel eyes and brought out the colour of a full, slightly pouting mouth. Kate bent her head forward and brushed her hair until her scalp tingled, tossing it back to let her hair fall wher-

ever it would. The results were a copper-
coloured cloud softly framing the perfect oval.
She was truly amazed with herself. She
couldn't remember ever looking this good
before. What would her friends and colleagues
in Brisbane say if she ever told them how much
time and trouble she had gone to, to discuss a
fence with a neighbour over a drink? But of
course she wouldn't tell them. She hardly
believed it herself.

Kate decided against taking the teddy bear.
Matthew would be asleep by now and she
wanted to see the expression on his face when
he received his gift.

She went the front way to the Hunter
mansion, the soft powdery sand cool under her
bare feet. The fresh sea air lifted her hair and
fanned her warm cheeks. Overhead, a black
sky played host to a trillion twinkling stars
while the rhythmic pounding of the waves
played the background music to which they
danced.

The patio was well lit. Kate stopped on the
flagstone steps leading up to it and slipped into
her high-heeled sandals. Gerard Hunter opened
the huge front door just as she was about to
bang the brass knocker. His inky blue eyes
swept over her, widening at her appearance.
Kate felt her blood stir and spread rapidly to
parts of her body she had never been aware of
before. The waves crashing on the beach grew

in volume, or so it seemed to her, as a loud roaring filled her ears. It came as a shock suddenly to realise she had outwitted herself. She had dressed for the man, hoping to soften his attitude towards her.

But now she realised Gerard Hunter was devouring her with his eyes. She felt like Little Red Riding Hood who had just delivered herself to the wolf. His eyes had darkened in colour as they lingered on her bare shoulders, moving slowly across to the swell of firm high breasts down to the trim waist and the gently rounded hips.

The seductive journey had taken mere seconds, but it was enough to strip Kate of her defences. She stood motionless in front of him. Her body felt on fire. It was a powerfully intoxicating experience and she trembled from the force of such an electrifying encounter.

He was speaking to her. Kate roused herself to take in what he was saying.

'You're spot on time.'

Her bemused eyes settled on his own wickedly cruel ones, the gleam in their depths mocking her. Snap out of it, an impatient voice inside her head rebuked her. She ran a trembling hand through her windswept hair, leaving it there while she slowly returned to earth and to precious sanity. Her voice was thick and very low and it sounded strange to her ears.

'Y-yes.' She took a deep breath in an attempt

to clear the potent vapours from her head. 'You did say eight o'clock.'

He nodded and reached for her hand, his strong brown fingers closing over hers as he led her in and shut the door. She looked down at the hand holding hers, noting how much deeper his tan was, how much bigger and stronger. She was conscious of a sudden desire to lift that hand and press it to her breast. She pulled abruptly away. Her eyes appeared almost totally green as they swept helplessly up to his face.

Long lashes partially veiled his eyes, hiding his expression, and for this Kate was grateful. Once again she had behaved like a schoolgirl, and what an idiot this man must think her. Thank goodness those lashes were so thick, so long; they hid the laughter which surely lurked behind.

He had dressed for the occasion as well. His dark hair brushed the edge of a crisp white shirt, the wine-coloured jacket unbuttoned, giving a casual elegance to broad shoulders and tapered waist. Cream-coloured trousers hugged well-muscled thighs while a pair of soft leather shoes completed the picture. His aftershave was a familiar scent by now and her delicate nostrils twitched as she breathed it in. She wondered if drops of it became lost in the deep cleft of his strong jaw, making the scent remain long after it should have gone. She wondered what it would feel like to touch that cleft.

Kate shook her head. Stop this madness! she told herself as he placed a strong hand on the small of her back and led her into the lounge.

'I'll be with you in a minute,' he said, bending his head close to her own, his breath fanning her cheek. 'I was in the process of getting Matthew to bed.' He glanced at his watch. 'A process which has been going on for almost two hours now,' and Kate smiled at the helpless tone in his voice and the look of complete exasperation in his dark blue eyes.

'Would you like me to help?' she suggested hopefully.

Matthew appeared as though on cue, and Kate's eyes melted at the sight of him. He was wearing red pyjamas and his black hair was rumpled. There was also a look of sheer defiance in his eyes. Kate could appreciate the look of exasperation in his father's eyes and the weariness in Mrs Abbott's!

Suddenly her view broadened, encompassing not only the small figure of Matthew and the much larger one of his father but of the whole room. The room was huge and could have been beautiful. Instead it seemed a lonely place, sparse, the expensive leather furnishings cold and rigid. A lovely stone fireplace dominated the room, but the hearth was bare, the yawning, gaping hole begging for a grate and a few pieces of wood. Beside the fireplace was a stack of framed pictures resting on the highly polished floor instead of where they belonged and her eyes swept over the bare, richly panelled walls. Somewhere from another part of the house there came the sound of a telephone. Gerard Hunter looked from Kate to his son.

'You can give it a try, but no more nonsense from you, young man,' he warned as he passed Matthew on his way towards the persistent sounds of the telephone. 'He's still on medication. It's on his bedside table,' he flung over his broad shoulder to Kate. 'The instructions are on the label.' His voice was brusque, businesslike and the rich baritone echoed in the still room as Kate and Matthew silently studied each other.

'Come on, then,' smiled Kate, reaching for Matthew's hand. 'Show me the way.'

Matthew silently led her up the winding staircase and down a long wide corridor. There was the same feeling of bleakness up here as there was below. Matthew's bedroom was like a dormitory and not at all like the gaily decorated rooms of Kate's little nephews. He sat on the edge of his bed and silently accepted his medicine, swallowing it dutifully. She tucked him in and smoothed back his hair, thinking how small and lonely he looked in this huge bare room. She bent and kissed his cheek and he sighed and closed his eyes.

'Sleep soundly, little Matthew,' she whispered gently before getting up and tiptoeing softly towards the door.

'That old Mr Kit-Kat is a nice cat, isn't he, Kate?'

Kate stopped in her tracks before spinning wildly around. Her eyes were huge in her face as she stared at the child.

'Matthew!' she gasped. 'You spoke! You can talk!'

''Course I can talk,' he muttered in disgust. 'What did you think? That I'm a baby?'

CHAPTER FOUR

KATE sat on the edge of Matthew's bed, her mind a whirl of confusion. Matthew lay back on his pillow, arms folded behind his dark head, a sad smile on his tortured little face.

'I had you fooled, huh?' he said in a small voice. 'You thought I couldn't talk.'

'I haven't known what to think,' Kate replied slowly, 'but I do know speech is a very precious thing.' She watched him closely. 'Why haven't you spoken to me before?'

Tears filled his eyes. 'I was afraid to.'

'Afraid?' Kate's smile was gentle. 'But you're not any more?'

'N-no,' he sniffed. 'You . . . you're my friend.'

'That's right,' Kate agreed softly. 'I'm your friend, Mrs Abbott is your friend and so is your daddy.'

'*No!*' Matthew shot up in his bed, his eyes wild. 'Just *you*, Kate. No one else!'

'Oh, Matthew,' Kate murmured, gathering his little body into her arms and gently rocking him. His arms crept round her neck while he sobbed out his misery and it was all Kate could do to keep from crying herself. Gradually the sobs subsided and he lay spent and exhausted in her arms. She lowered him back on to his pillow and wiped his face with tissues from his bedside table. Her movements were slow and gentle, her manner calm. She thought of the teddy bear and wished she had brought it. Matthew was in desperate need of being cuddled and to cuddle.

He had been deeply hurt! Kate could see that now. She could see it and she had felt it. The same applied to his father. They were both hurting and neither knew how to handle it. Matthew's escape had been his silence; Gerard's his bitterness. A strangled sob tore from the child's throat and went straight to her heart.

She stayed with him until he drifted into sleep. Her eyes were filled with concern as she gazed tenderly down at him. He had spoken to her, he considered her to be his friend. She touched his cheek, stroked the soft warm skin and smoothed back his hair before she finally left him.

Kate stood outside Matthew's room, her back pressed against the door. How was she going to tell Gerard that his son had spoken to her? Would he be glad the silence had finally broken or would he resent the fact that his son had chosen her as his confidante? If the latter, then his bitterness would grow and this would be bad for Matthew, for himself and for her.

She sighed heavily and made her way down the long corridor. The mingling odours of fresh paint, plaster and wood filled her nostrils. Everything was so new, so cold and damp-feeling. Why would Gerard build such an enormous house? she couldn't help but wonder, as she passed several doors, some of them open leading to bare rooms, a few closed. The overhead chandeliers cast a cold glare on the bare walls and floors. No wonder Matthew had found it easy maintaining his role of silence in such a coldly forbidding place!

She paused on the landing of the circular staircase. The staircase swept through the centre of this huge mansion and on either side, separated by another wide corridor below, were the other rooms. From where Kate stood she could see into the lounge, the dining room and several other rooms which were as yet unfurnished. Lights were on or off at random as though nobody much cared one way or the other. A shaft of light appeared from under one of the closed doors and when she got closer she was amazed to hear the sounds of office machinery coming from behind it. She tapped softly and then opened the door.

Her eyes widened in amazement. Sophisticated computers lined one wall, green, red and yellow lights flashing wildly. A Telex machine was in the process of delivering a message, the white paper folding into Gerard Hunter's large

brown hands. He had discarded his jacket and
rolled up the sleeves of his white shirt, his
deeply tanned arms in startling contrast to the
snowy white of the fabric. His black hair was
in wild disarray as though each strand had been
personally dealt with by those long, tapering
fingers. A deep flush stained his high cheekbones, adding even more colour to the dark
hue of his skin. Blue-black eyes blazed down
at the message he was reading. The telephone
call he had received earlier had obviously been
the catalyst which had sparked him into a
human dynamo.

He ripped the message from the machine and
Kate watched, fascinated, as his long brown
fingers moved rapidly over the keyboard typing
out a reply. Kate stepped into the office and
softly closed the door behind her. He glanced
up and saw her, startled, and she smiled. He
straightened and dragged a weary hand through
his hair and down to his neck, kneading the
stiff muscles there.

'Ah, Kate, I'm sorry, I got waylaid.' With
incredible ease he dropped out of his com-
mercial world and slipped into his domestic
one. 'How's Matthew? In bed and asleep, I
hope?'

She loved the way he had somehow turned
her plain-sounding name into one of sophisticated charm. Her beautiful mouth lifted in a
smile. 'Yes, Matthew is asleep.'

Black brows arched in surprise. 'So soon? You must have a magic touch.'

'It is after nine o'clock,' she reminded him gently.

Gerard glanced at his watch. 'So it is.' Blue eyes swept over her and she felt that now familiar surge of warmth coursing through her body. His eyes took on a dangerous quality. 'You must think me a bore,' he rebuked himself, placing a warm hand under her chin to lift her face. 'I invited you for drinks and then left you to care for my son.'

Kate stared helplessly into his eyes. 'No, I don't think that,' she heard herself say. Her eyes moved down to his mouth. 'I enjoyed putting Matthew to bed.'

His hand swept around to the nape of her neck, his fingers splaying through her hair. He drew her closer.

'Did you?' he whispered hoarsely.

'Y-yes,' she whispered back, and for the life of her she couldn't remember what they were talking about. All she knew was that her body was on fire and that her heart seemed to be everywhere at once. Gerard's dark head slowly descended, his mouth hovering above hers until only a whisper separated them. Their lips touched in a fiery explosion. Gerard withdrew immediately, looked her fully in the face with eyes darkened by desire and then pulled her to him, his hands moulding her against the hard contours of his body while his mouth covered hers.

Suddenly Kate knew this was what she had been waiting for, what she had wanted since the first time she had laid eyes on Gerard Hunter. He held her to him, drinking in her sweetness like a man who had tasted only bitterness and wanted to rid himself of the taste.

She felt his hands against her, holding her to him, and a thrill shot through her. His kiss became deeper and Kate wrapped her arms around his neck, her fingers brushing through the thickness of his hair, holding on to him as if she could never let him go.

Gerard's mouth left hers to burn a fiery trail across her jaw, her neck, nibbling gently at her earlobe until she was quivering. She bent her head back, her hands on the sides of his face as his mouth moved slowly down to her bare shoulders.

'Kate!' he groaned feverishly, raising his head to look into her flushed face, her lids lowered in smoky passion. 'I'm sorry.' He set her away from him, dragging a rueful hand through his hair. 'I don't know what got into me. I don't usually ravish young ladies.'

He was visibly shaken by what had happened, but Kate managed to appear quite calm. She should have *known* it would be like this between them. After all, her body had given her plenty of warning. He only had to look at her and it sparked off the fire within her. Even now, if he touched her, she felt she would become a willing slave in his arms. She was totally defenceless against him. Their body chemistries were dangerous. She could still feel the tiny explosions in every part of her being, the lingering fires burning in her veins.

'I'm twenty-six years old,' she reminded him, her voice sounding breathless. 'I've been working and living on my own for years. Does that still qualify me as a *young* lady?'

His blue eyes widened at her words and then hardened visibly. 'You're offering yourself to me, is that it? You want me to know you're a woman of the world?'

Kate's cheeks flushed a fiery red. She hadn't imagined such a typically male response would come from his lips. She smothered a sigh.

'I'm not in the habit of offering myself to anyone, Gerard,' she stated calmly. 'Do I look like a sacrificial lamb to you?'

The hard look disappeared as he studied her. Her head was thrown back, the pert chin thrust forward and there was a wisdom in those large hazel eyes which left no doubt that Kate Chalmers was indeed her own person. His body relaxed, the hard lines in his face softened and to her astonishment he actually grinned. Kate felt her heart expand in her chest and then somersault to her throat. Her mouth went dry and she swallowed convulsively.

'You look . . .' Gerard shoved his hands into his trouser pockets. 'Never mind how you look!' he growled, and turned away.

The Telex machine came to life again, claiming his full attention. Twenty minutes passed as he received and sent out messages.

'What is all this?' Kate asked as soon as the room became quiet.

'My work,' he replied nonchalantly. 'I have an oil firm and this is its nerve centre. We're drilling on the north-west coast. Messages come in here and I relay them to my branches in Brisbane and Melbourne.' He gave her a crooked smile. 'But enough about that. I haven't forgotten I promised you a drink.' He placed a warm hand on the small of her back and led her from the room, closing the door on the flashing lights and the clattering machines.

'What will it be?' he asked as they entered the lounge.

'Sherry will be fine,' Kate answered. She watched as he poured the drinks, sherry for her and Scotch for himself, before they settled themselves on one of the soft leather sofas. A small frown puckered her smooth brow as she wondered how she should tell him about Matthew.

'You will be pleased to know I've decided against a six-foot fence,' he surprised Kate by saying. 'So you can wipe that worried frown from your face. It spoils your beauty.'

Kate leaned against the back of the sofa. She closed her eyes, her long golden-tipped lashes brushing against her cheeks. The fence had lost its importance compared to what she had to say! Gerard moved closer beside her and she felt his thigh brushing against hers, the contact spreading a delicious warmth throughout her body. Her eyes flew open, when he touched her cheek, to be arrested immediately by his own midnight-blue orbs. His breath fanned her cheeks smelling faintly of the expensive Scotch. Her eyes swayed down to the dark sensuous mouth and she trembled as his lips lightly brushed her own.

'Why would I put up a fence to keep you out?' he said huskily, and Kate knew he was asking the question of himself and not of her. His hand traced the outline of her breast.

'You're so very beautiful, Kate,' he murmured, and she gasped with pleasure as his mouth caressed her skin.

'Gerard!' Her voice sounded strangled and he raised his head in genuine surprise. She slipped away from him, her cheeks crimson as she bowed her head, and struggled to gain composure. It was all happening too fast.

His own face fused with colour, dangerous glints showing beneath lowered lids. 'What's wrong?' he growled suspiciously. 'How can you just switch off like that?'

'I'm not, I . . .' Kate gazed at him helplessly.

Her body was clamouring for his touch, her fingertips ached for the feel of him, her lips longed for his.

'Don't bother explaining,' he said harshly, springing to his feet to glare down at her. 'I should have held out a little longer about the fence!' He reached for her hand and yanked her to her feet. 'You got what you came for.' He pulled her roughly towards him. 'If there's anything else you want, let me know.' His hands slid down to her hips, pinning her against his hard body. 'We'll negotiate,' he muttered thickly, releasing her.

Kate backed away from him, her hand against her mouth. 'Gerard, please, please don't look at me like that!' He thought she had betrayed him, that she had used her body to get her way with the fence. 'I . . . I——' Kate took a deep breath. 'Gerard, please sit down,' and she again took her place on the sofa and patted the cushion beside her. A loud snort filled the room as he looked at her with scorn. She quickly pulled her hand from the cushion and clasped it with the other on her lap.

'Matthew spoke to me tonight,' she said quietly.

The softly spoken words seemed to echo in the large room, hitting Gerard with such force that his breath was knocked out of him in a shuddering sigh. The sound went straight to Kate's heart.

An awful silence filled the room. Kate watched in horror as Gerard seemed to crumple in front of her. The proud broad shoulders stooped, the ramrod-straight back bent and his head fell forward. He thrust trembling hands into his pockets.

'Gerard,' Kate whispered hoarsely. 'Please, Gerard. Sit down and I'll tell you about it.'

Bleak eyes found her own. 'Gloat about it is what you mean, isn't it?'

Shocked, Kate shook her head. 'I would never gloat about a thing like that, Gerard.'

Slowly he sat down beside her, shoulders and back stooped forward, hands and arms dangling between his legs. She longed to comfort him, to hold him in her arms the way she had done to Matthew, but she knew this was not the moment. Her words had hurt him terribly, when she had prayed they would make him glad, fill him with relief, make him want to rejoice.

'He spoke about old Mr Kit-Kat and he asked if I could be his friend,' Kate continued quietly, fighting back tears at the look of anguish in Gerard's eyes.

He turned slowly and her heart cried in protest at the naked misery in his face.

'My son hates me, did you know that?' he whispered hoarsely.

'*No!*' Kate grabbed his hands. 'You mustn't think that, you mustn't believe it!'

His laugh was bitter. 'It's the truth.' He looked down at her small hands holding his. 'I knew Matthew liked you,' he sighed. 'He was always trying to get over to your place and I must admit I resented the fact that he preferred your company to mine.' Gerard turned her hands around, his thumbs lightly caressing her moist palms. 'I guess I was jealous.' He smiled sheepishly, a deep hurt lingering in his eyes. 'I lived for the moment when he would give me a hug and call me Dad. It seems so long since I've heard him say that,' he finished brokenly.

Kate felt shattered. Gerard's hurt ran deeper than she had imagined. He was grieving, actually grieving for his son. Matthew was barely more than a baby. How could a baby wound his father so deeply, destroy so thoroughly? Only Gerard could answer this, and she hoped that when he was ready he would unburden himself to her. In the meantime she had earned their trust, and it was more than she had counted on. She would be content with this, and when Gerard lifted her hands to his lips she sighed. Whatever the storm, she would face it with them.

Gerard suddenly stiffened and Kate followed his glance to the lounge entrance. Matthew stood there, his silent glare focused on his father. Kate tried to pull her hands from Gerard's, but he only tightened his grip.

'Be still,' he warned in a low voice. 'Let me

handle this.' He smiled across to his son. 'What is it, Matt? Can't sleep?'

Matthew stepped into the room, his glance going from his father to Kate, finally settling on Kate. Kate held her breath. His small face was pinched in anger.

'You're supposed to be *my* friend, my *best* friend!' he shrieked. 'Why are you sitting so close to *him?*'

'That's enough, Matthew,' his father warned. 'Kate *is* your friend, she told me so.' He rose to his feet and crossed the room to his son. Matthew glared up at him, a small figure of fury. 'Kate and I are friends, too,' Gerard added gently.

'No, you're not!' Matthew wailed. 'You want to take her away from me!'

Kate watched, horrified, as Matthew started kicking Gerard in the shins, his small bare feet lashing out while tiny fists flailed against Gerard's thighs. Gerard picked Matthew up and slung him over his shoulder, the child kicking and screaming all the way up the stairs. Kate covered her ears with her hands, but Matthew's agonised screams penetrated to the very core of her being. She heard a door slam upstairs and then all was quiet.

When Gerard returned Kate was still sitting exactly where he had left her. Her eyes seemed huge in her pale face.

'Thank you for waiting,' he said quietly,

dragging a weary hand through his thick black hair. 'He's finally asleep.'

Kate sat motionless, her hands clasped tightly in her lap. 'Will he be all right?' she asked worriedly.

'Eventually,' he said flatly, and Kate knew he was emotionally spent. He didn't join her on the sofa, standing instead by the fireplace, his back facing her, his hands spread across the mantelpiece. Slowly he turned, his eyes filled with agony. 'You have a right to know what this . . . that . . . was all about.'

Kate shook her head in protest, but he silenced her with an impatient wave of his hand. 'You wanted to get involved, so you may as well know what you're up against.' She was shaken by his tone but knew he was right. She *had* done her utmost to get involved.

'My wife and I were divorced six months ago,' he began bitterly. 'I was given custody of Matthew mainly because Ria didn't want a four-year-old cramping her lifestyle. She promised to visit him regularly, to take him out——' He shook his dark head. 'Promises she had no intention of keeping.' Pity filled his eyes. 'Matthew kept finding excuses for her; she was sick, she was away. Every weekend he waited.'

Gerard crossed the room to refill their glasses, placing Kate's beside her on the end table. The light from the lamp caught the hard planes of his face, outlining the strong jaw and high cheekbones. He glanced at her, his eyes seeming to go straight through her, and she wondered if it was another woman he was really seeing. A pain caught in her chest. Was Gerard still in love with his ex-wife?

He sat down next to her on the wide plush sofa, long legs stretched out, the glass of Scotch held loosely in his tanned hands. His eyes were focused on the golden liquid as he continued talking. 'I decided to get Matt away from Melbourne. I remembered this place when I visited the Boyntons here several years ago. Matt and I flew up, checked it out and made arrangements for this house to be built. Matt was taken with the idea of living right on the beach, and I thought everything would be all right. The divorce had been rough on him . . .' Gerard leaned forward, clasping the glass so tightly in his strong hands, Kate feared it would shatter. 'I told Ria we were moving, she didn't object, but the day we were to leave she turned up, threw a tantrum and accused me of stealing her child.' Gerard cleared his throat and Kate placed her hand on his arm, her fingers pressing into his hard flesh. 'Matthew became hysterical,' he continued, his eyes tortured at the memory. 'For once in his young life he truly believed his mummy wanted him, that she had finally grown to love him.' Gerard buried his head in his hands and his shoulders shook. 'Ria knew I wouldn't tell him the truth.

She didn't want him. It was her own misguided way of getting back at me.'

Kate remained silent, horrified by what she was hearing. She had to swallow several times before she was able to speak.

'Afterwards, when Ria had gone, was that when Matthew retreated into his silent world?'

Gerard ran his hands roughly over his face. 'Yes. He seemed to go into a trance. I took him to a doctor.' He laughed bitterly. 'And he told me my four-year-old son was suffering from a nervous breakdown brought on by severe trauma!'

Kate felt sick all over. 'I'm sorry,' she whispered, placing her head against Gerard's shoulder.

Without warning Gerard sprang to his feet. Kate stared helplessly up at him while he glared down at her.

'Sorry?' Again that horribly bitter laugh. 'Is our story too sordid for the aspiring reporter? Do you wish now you'd minded your own business? Did you think Matthew had been born a mute and that you'd somehow performed a major miracle?' he rasped.

'Stop!' Kate jumped to her feet. 'Stop torturing yourself, Gerard, and for goodness' sake stop feeling sorry for yourself!'

He stared at her in wild-eyed disbelief. 'I'm not——'

'You are!' she broke in hurriedly. 'Your

heart has been broken too. Oh, maybe not by your wife but by watching Matthew suffer and believing you weren't doing enough to help him.' Her voice became softer and she smiled up at him. 'But obviously you've done a great deal. Matthew is talking *and* screaming! Day by day, bit by bit you've managed to restore his faith in life.'

Gerard shook his head and stuffed his hands into his pockets. 'I know what you're trying to do, Kate,' he smiled sadly, 'but it won't work. You heard him. He's even afraid I'll take you from him!'

Kate reached up to place a tender hand on his cheek. 'Then we'll have to prove him wrong, won't we? We'll become the Three Musketeers. All for one and one for all.'

Gerard pressed her hand to his mouth, his eyes lingering on her upturned face. Then almost savagely he brushed it away. 'I've been part of a threesome,' he ground out bitterly, 'and you've seen the results!'

Kate shrank from the contempt in his eyes. Horrified, she realised she had her answer. Gerard had given everything just as she had suspected, but Ria, his ex-wife, hadn't finished with him yet!

CHAPTER FIVE

KATE awoke to the sounds of voices outside her bedroom windows. She cast a bleary eye to the little alarm clock on her bedside table. Seven o'clock. Yesterday that would have been late. She was usually down at the beach by this time. Today it meant she had very little sleep, having spent until the small hours of the morning going over the events of the night before.

Gerard had walked her the short distance home, depositing her on the doorstep and looking down at her with a deep unhappiness still lingering in his eyes. She had longed to comfort him, to cast away his problems with a magic wand.

'Kate,' he had whispered, taking her in his arms, and she clung to him the way she had when she had almost drowned.

'You'll see,' she had whispered softly. 'Everything will be okay,' and he had drawn her closer into the harbour of his breast.

He had left her then and Kate had watched as he slowly made his way back to his cold mansion. When she finally crawled into bed she thought of Ria, wondering what that woman was doing at that very moment, and if sleep came easily to her.

The voices were getting louder now and Kate moaned, tossing the pillow she had put over her head to muffle the sounds, on to the floor. Suddenly she sat up, ears alert. A child's voice mingled with that of a man's. She sprang to her feet and put her head out the window.

Gerard was standing by the old fence dressed in a pair of black shorts and a black singlet. Perspiration gleamed on his tanned muscular shoulders and in his hand was a spade. Beside him sat Matthew dressed similarly in blue shorts and white T-shirt. His knees were drawn up to his chin and his small arms were wrapped around his legs. Kate couldn't make out the expression on his face. He didn't look happy, but then he didn't look especially miserable. She had the feeling he was experiencing both emotions but couldn't decide which one he should nurture.

'Hi, guys!' she sang out gaily.

Both turned to look at her. A grin spread slowly across Gerard's face at the sight of her poking her head out the little window, while Matthew merely looked at her, his little face pinched and pale, his eyes slightly swollen from the crying he had done the night before.

Gerard waved the spade at her. 'Hi, yourself. Don't tell me we woke you up?' he asked in feigned innocence.

'Oh, no,' she drawled, taking her cue from

Gerard and entering into the spirit of things. 'What are you two up to?' Her eyes rested on some rotten pieces of board lying by Gerard's feet. 'Hey, that's some of my fence!'

'Matt and I decided you needed a new fence. Isn't that right, son?'

Matthew nodded uninterestedly while he nibbled at a blade of grass. Kate caught the look of despair in Gerard's eyes as he watched his son.

'What kind of new fence?' Kate asked enthusiastically while she felt her heart lurch painfully in her chest.

'Tell her, Matt.'

Matthew sighed. 'Same as the one you've already got.'

Kate pretended to be horrified. 'Not the same as that rickety old thing!' she gasped.

''Course not,' Matthew said in disgust. 'It's gonna be a new one and it's gonna be little and it's gonna be painted white.'

'A little white picket fence!' exclaimed Kate. 'Why, that sounds wonderful!'

'And that's not all it's gonna have,' Matthew continued importantly. 'Guess what else it's gonna have?'

Kate wrinkled her brow as she tried to think. Finally she gave up. 'I can't,' she sighed.

'It's gonna have a little gate for me so I can visit you whenever I like.' Suddenly he giggled. 'You look like Mopsy poking your head out of the window.' He looked up at his father. 'Doesn't Kate look like Mopsy, Daddy?'

Gerard looked at Kate, his eyes holding hers while her smooth complexion burned a fiery red. She knew Matthew's description was fairly accurate. Her copper-coloured hair was always a mass of unruly curls first thing in the morning and after tossing and turning most of the night it was safe to assume it was even worse today. Her faded old pink nightie probably completed the picture, she thought, as Gerard continued to stare at her, a faint gleam in his eyes.

'She does at that,' he drawled, eyes darkened in amusement.

Kate poked her tongue out at them before drawing her curtains in a pretended rage. A grin spread slowly across her face as she heard Matthew's giggles mingling with Gerard's low rumbling chuckles. It didn't take her long to have a quick shower and slip into a pair of white shorts and matching white top before she was outside.

Gerard came immediately over to her and took her hand. 'Thanks for going along with this,' he said quietly so Matthew couldn't hear, indicating the fence behind them with a nod of his dark head. 'I needed a project Matthew could help me with. The fence seemed ideal. It's on neutral ground and it's something we can share without complications. You'll be the buffer between us, Kate, so act naturally and put up whatever objections you can think of.'

She grinned happily. 'So you and Matt can convince me, right?'

Gerard smiled down at her, his eyes lingering on the exquisite beauty of her face. 'Right,' he agreed, giving her hand a conspiratorial squeeze before leading her over to join Matthew sitting by the fence.

'The Three Musketeers, eh?' Kate grinned happily at them both. 'So you think I need a new fence.'

Gerard nodded and grinned back. 'We agreed there wouldn't be a six-foot-high fence,' he stated calmly, blue eyes gleaming down at her upturned face. 'But this rickety old thing has to go.'

'A little white picket fence,' Matthew repeated his earlier description, 'with a gate for me so's I can visit you without having to find a hole to get through.'

'It will be the same as you had before,' Gerard continued where his son had left off. 'The same height and style.' His grin broadened. 'Well, what do you think?'

Kite pretended to consider. She placed her hands on her hips and looked from Gerard to his son. 'I don't know,' she said. 'I sort of like this old one. My grandparents built it, you know.'

Gerard put his arm around her shoulders and hugged her to him. 'And so it's high time it was replaced.'

Kate looked at Matthew. 'Do you think we could do it?' she asked. 'Do you think the three of us could really build a brand-new fence?'

Matthew bobbed his head up and down. ''Course we can!' he said, thrusting out his little chest. 'I've even got my own tools,' and he held out a toy set for Kate to see.

Kate took the tools and examined each one carefully while Matthew watched with unconcealed pride. 'I got them last Christmas,' he told her, 'but I've never had a chance to use them, not until now. Do you like them, Kate?' he asked anxiously. 'Do you think they'll do the job?'

Kate handed them back to him. 'They're lovely tools,' she said, smilingly. 'But I think I'm jealous, Matt. All I've got is a rusty old hammer!'

'You can use mine,' Matthew assured her quickly. He turned to his father. 'Did you hear that, Dad? Kate's only got a rusty old hammer, so I said she could use mine.'

Gerard placed his hand on his son's head. 'That's very kind of you, son,' he declared solemnly, his eyes meeting and holding Kate's. 'Shall we get started?'

'But won't it be expensive?' asked Kate, thinking of her rather meagre savings account. 'I think it's only fair to warn you guys, what you see standing before you is a very poor lady.'

Gerard chuckled and placed a long finger over her lips. 'The fence isn't going to cost either of us a cent.'

She took his finger away and held on to it. 'It isn't? But how?'

'There's plenty of wood left over from the construction of my place along with nails and paint. The only thing it's going to cost us is sore backs.' He grinned down at her. 'Now, doesn't that sound like great fun?'

Kate pretended to be horrified. 'Sore backs? Hard work? On my holiday?'

'Well, I'll be giving you plenty of breaks; an hour off for lunch, ten minutes for morning and afternoon smokes.' His easy grin swept over her.

Kate's eyes were radiant. It would be fun, the three of them working together. As Gerard's finger slowly traced the outline of her mouth with the finger she was still holding, she knew that if he had suggested it she would willingly have agreed to the cottage being torn down just to be with him as he built it up again.

'Should we get started, Daddy?' asked Matthew, anxious to begin.

Kate and Gerard laughed at his eagerness. 'I doubt if Kate has had breakfast,' Gerard said, ruffling Matthew's hair. 'And we can't expect her to work on an empty stomach. Run over to our place and see if Mrs Abbott has got any of those blueberry muffins left over.'

'She has, I saw her put them away. I counted six. Should I bring them all over?' he asked eagerly.

'I think so, son, we've got to feed this lady if we expect any work from her. And ask Mrs Abbott if she would be kind enough to make up a jug of lemonade.' He looked up at the cloudless blue sky. 'It's going to be hot, we'll need plenty to drink.'

Matthew scampered off, pleased with his mission, and Kate turned excited eyes to Gerard. 'What happened?' she asked breathlessly. 'Last night you spoke of miracles, and I believe I've seen one.'

'I can't believe it myself,' Gerard admitted. 'After I got back from your place last night, I went upstairs to my bedroom. Matthew was sound asleep on my bed. I sat down beside him. He woke up and we found ourselves just looking at each other, neither of us saying a word. Suddenly he was in my lap and he cried his little heart out. I just held him, I didn't know what else to do. When he stopped crying he asked me all sorts of questions about the divorce and what it really meant, and most of all if it had been his fault.'

'Poor kid,' Kate said softly, her eyes clouding.

'Not any more,' Gerard disagreed. 'We had a long talk, a talk which should have happened ages ago, only I thought he was too young to understand. I was wrong. He desperately needed reassurance that he was in no way responsible for what happened between Ria and me.' He looked down at her. 'He's quite a kid, my little Matt.'

Kate readily agreed and snuggled closer into Gerard's arms, her head resting against his chest listening to the steady beats of his heart. 'He takes after his father,' she murmured, wondering why the mention of Ria's name should always distress her so.

When Matthew came back with the muffins and lemonade, Kate was made to eat three and drink two glasses of lemonade before they pronounced her fit to begin work.

An hour after they started Kate and Matthew were pulled from the workforce and made to sit on an old log while Gerard bandaged their bruised thumbs. He stood in front of them looking down at their hot faces, and shook his head mournfully. 'What a pair!' he drawled, while Kate and Matthew held up their bandaged thumbs with self-pity in their eyes.

It took almost a month to pull up the old fence and build the new one. A month of fun, laughter, sweat and more than the occasional tear when hammers repeatedly hit the wrong nail! During that time, Kate learnt a lot about Gerard, and day by day her respect and admiration for him grew.

His patience was remarkable. Not only with Matthew but with Kate herself. Several times Kate and Matthew crept off to hide behind the bushes, their hands muffling their laughter as Gerard worked on convinced they were toiling behind him. When it was discovered they were missing, he would make a great show of searching for them, looking everywhere except where they were, finding them at last while they held their sides and laughed helplessly. He would break a leafy branch from a tree and chase them back to work, while their squeals of laughter brought Mrs Abbott running out to see what was going on.

They were having the time of their lives. Kate showed Matthew how to feed the rosellas and how to mix their special brew. Old Mr Kit-Kat came each day for his snack and Matthew would stretch out on his tummy and watch the cat lap his milk and nibble his food.

During the worst heat of the day between eleven and two, Gerard would call a halt and the trio would race down to the ocean and frolic in the surf. Lunch was always under the sprawling poinciana tree in Kate's garden, and while Matthew snoozed afterwards under the shade of the brilliant scarlet blossoms, she and Gerard would talk, often finding themselves in each other's arms, their bodies clamouring for total fulfilment. She had never given herself to a man, and now she understood why. No one had ever come close to making her feel the way Gerard did. She loved him.

She would have given herself gladly to him, but he was the one holding back. The evenings after Matthew was in bed would end with Gerard pulling away from her, leaving her feeling miserable and frustrated. While they talked openly and freely about every other subject under the sun, they never discussed this. Kate was afraid to. She was terrified Gerard might still be in love with his ex-wife. So frightened was she of this possibility that she didn't dare ask herself why this should matter.

But Mrs Abbott knew what Kate was afraid to admit. Kate had fallen hopelessly in love with Gerard Hunter! Always pretty, Kate was now beautiful. She was, in fact, radiant. Her eyes lit up whenever he entered the room; and she clung to his every word, always wanting to be near him, touching him, doing things for him. In the evenings, Mrs Abbott would poke her head into the enormous lounge before she left for home, and the scene was always the same. Gerard would be reading aloud from a story book with Matthew on his lap and his arm around Kate. Kate's head would be nestled against his chest, her eyes half closed as though hypnotised by his rich deep baritone voice.

While Gerard was responsible for the changes in Kate, Kate had been responsible for some changes too. The big house now had a charm it had lacked before. Pictures had been hung and scattered rugs now softened the effect of bare wooden floors. Matthew's bedroom had been completely redecorated with gaily printed wallpaper and bright new furniture. The teddy bear she had given him had pride of place on his bed.

'My holiday will soon be over,' Kate told Gerard one evening as she watched him sort out papers on his desk in his workroom.

He glanced up and smiled. She was wearing a thin cotton dress, the fabric hugging the slender curves of her body. Her rich copper-coloured hair was pulled back and fastened with a yellow ribbon the same colour as her dress. The smooth flawless skin was without make-up, giving her a gentle vulnerability which matched her wistful tone. Her soft hazel eyes were sad.

'When?'

She swallowed hard. 'I have to start work on Monday.'

He straightened slowly from his desk, his eyes darkening. 'So soon?'

Kate nodded and sighed. 'I've had nearly six weeks.'

A muscle jumped alongside his jaw. 'You can't ask for more time off?'

She shook her head and this time the sigh was longer. 'No, I've taken all I could.' She attempted a laugh. 'I owe them time now.'

Gerard dragged his hand through his hair and she smiled at the instant mess.

'I. . . Matthew will miss you.' A crooked smile followed the words. 'He'll be lost. He won't know what to do with himself.'

What about you? Kate pleaded silently.

'I'll miss him too,' she answered quietly. 'But I'll keep in touch.'

Gerard gave her a searching look. 'When will you be back?'

She shrugged. 'I don't know. Not before Christmas.'

'Kate, I . . .' His voice trailed off.

'Yes?' She moved closer to him. 'What is it, Gerard?'

'Nothing.' He stuffed his hands into his pockets.

'Will you be here for Christmas?' she asked.

'Yes.'

'Gerard, I . . .' Her voice trailed away like his had done.

He looked at her sharply, dark brows raised above clear, blue eyes, holding hers.

'Yes, what is it, Kate?'

Her glance fell. 'N-nothing.' To her horror she felt tears burning at the back of her eyes and she quickly blinked them away.

He placed his hand under her chin and gently lifted it. 'You don't appear to be too happy about going back.'

She forced a smile. 'It's leaving Bargara that does it,' she insisted. 'All this peace and beauty.' The tears were threatening her again and her eyes glistened. 'I'll be all right once I get back to work.'

A scowl darkened his face. 'Why couldn't you have an ordinary job like a secretary or a teacher or a nurse? Why must you be a reporter?'

They had discussed Kate's job many times and in the beginning she had made it sound far more exciting than it actually was, adding danger and drama to her accounts. Gerard had become so concerned for her safety that she had finally admitted the truth, sheepishly confessing that her assignments mainly covered the social scenes—weddings, ballets and the occasional rock group. It had been mention of the rock groups which Gerard hadn't liked and still didn't. She gave him a tremulous smile.

'It's what I'm trained to do,' she answered, smoothing the scowl from his face with feather-soft hands. 'I guess I'm too old to learn another trade and a girl's got to eat. Besides, I enjoy it.'

He took her hands and pressed the palms to his lips, a brooding expression in his eyes.

'I'll miss you, Kate.'

She swallowed hard. 'I'll miss you, too,' she answered simply.

Kate started missing Gerard and Matthew

before she had even left Bargara. The last few days of her holiday were spent wondering how she was ever going to manage until she returned. Every moment spent with them was precious, and in the evenings when she and Gerard were alone she committed to memory every detail of his face.

When at last the day came for her to leave, Gerard and Matthew were there to see her off.

'You won't forget to come back, will you, Kate?' Matthew asked anxiously while he bravely fought back tears.

Kate hugged him. 'I'll be here for Christmas, you can count on it.'

'That's not so far away, is it, Kate? You're sure you'll be back then?'

'I'm sure,' she promised solemnly, kneeling down and pulling him into her arms. Over the top of his head she caught the look in Gerard's eyes and her heart twisted painfully in her chest. She knew he was remembering another woman who had promised Matthew the very same thing!

Kate rose shakily to her feet and held a trembling hand towards Gerard. His body had stiffened and there was dark censure in his eyes. *I'm not Ria!* Kate's eyes silently pleaded with him and gradually the harshness left his face and he took her hand, gently pulling her to him, his arms tightening around her as if he was afraid to let her go. It was at that moment, with her ear against his chest listening to the frantic beat of his heart, that Kate realised just how much she loved him.

She felt a surge of joy sweep through her body. Every part of her tingled with new awareness. She wanted to laugh and shout for joy. She wanted to grab Gerard's hands and dance with him like gypsies around the garden. Her body trembled with the force.

She threw back her head to look her love in the face, and he stared down at her astonishing beauty, the feverish excitement in her eyes and a guarded look crept into his own.

'Gerard,' Kate whispered dreamily. 'Oh, Gerard, I . . .'

'Sssh!' he broke in, silencing her. 'Don't say it, Kate. Don't!'

'But . . .' She didn't finish, there was no need to. A horrible chill crept over her heart, icy-cold needles bursting her bubble of happiness. She felt cloaked in despair as reality hit her in the stomach, making her feel quite nauseated. Gerard didn't love her and was saving her from making a fool of herself by confessing that she loved him.

He set her away, his broad hands clasping her shoulders. 'Have a safe journey, Kate,' he said gruffly.

Kate nodded and smiled bravely. All she wanted now was to get away. Somehow she managed to give Matthew another hug and when she felt his tears against her cheek and his little arms around her neck, she had to bite hard on her own trembling lips to keep from crying herself.

But Matthew sensed the change in her and with a child's instinct knew something was wrong. He refused to let her go, clinging to her legs, his old insecurities raging to the surface as he clung pathetically to her. Gerard had to prise him loose and Kate stood helplessly by the car, her face etched in misery as Gerard signalled for her to leave.

She didn't want to. How could she go while Matthew was so upset, while *she* was so miserable? Pain tore at her heart. If only Gerard would accept her love, trust in her, then she wouldn't feel as she did now, as though she could breathe in but not out. She was suffocating!

'Gerard . . . Matthew,' she said hoarsely, her hands outstretched as she moved the few steps towards them, but Gerard shook his dark head brusquely and his eyes warned her off. It was all too much for Kate. A strange sound tore from her throat and then she found herself behind the wheel of her car, her hand shaking as she started the ignition and the unreal feeling, tearing from the driveway, as though she couldn't quite believe she had left her loved ones, that they had *let* her leave!

Gerard's warning blue eyes and Matthew's

pathetic sobs chased her through the seemingly endless fields of swaying sugar cane, through the leafy streets of Bundaberg, past the quaint old town of Childers and on and on until the flat canefields gave way to the rolling green hills of Gympie where some still believed there was the promise of gold in the distant hills.

The painful lump in her throat stayed with her until at last she found herself at her flat. She dragged her suitcase from the boot of the car and fitted her key in the lock, opening the door. Her eyes moved slowly around the lounge. Everything appeared the same, exactly as she had left it.

There was the magazine she had been reading the evening before she had left for her holiday still on the beige sofa. In the pretty pink and white kitchen she found the glass she had rinsed and left standing on the draining board. In the bathroom was the bright yellow towel she had used after her shower and placed over the rail to dry. The only change had been in herself.

Kate wandered slowly back to the lounge, picked up her suitcase and carried it into her bedroom. The familiar bed greeted her, the cover matching the pale blue curtains hanging against latticed windows. Her flat was beautiful. She had lived in it for five years now and had decorated it herself. It had been her refuge and her sanctuary, a safe harbour to enter after a particularly stormy day when nothing had seemed to go right. It was a good place to be now!

Or was it? Kate sat down on the edge of the bed and tried desperately to rid herself of that painful lump in her throat before it managed to choke her. Perhaps a cup of tea might help.

Sitting at the kitchen table with her elbows propped on the surface and her hands holding her chin, she stared down at the dark liquid in her cup. Finally she forced herself to take a sip of the steaming hot liquid. She coughed and almost choked while tears scalded her eyes. She gave in to them, letting them drip down the sides of her cheeks and splash on to the table. She wept silently for several minutes, but the tears weren't enough to wash away her despair.

She had been a fool to let herself fall in love with Gerard, she realised that now. But it was too late to do anything about it. She loved him with her whole heart, her whole being. She couldn't just switch off her feelings as if nothing had happened. But Gerard didn't want her, didn't want her love! Her shoulders shook with helpless sobs. He knew she was going to say she loved him, he *knew* it, but he hadn't wanted to hear the words.

But surely he had felt something. Kate refused to believe he hadn't. She had felt him tremble in her arms, had felt his desire and his urgency. She had marvelled at his control and knew what it had cost him. And all along she had thought he hadn't committed that final act out of respect for her because he had been married and divorced and he considered her an innocent. She had thought he hadn't wanted to take advantage of her.

That was what she had thought, but now of course she knew the truth: Gerard simply didn't care enough for her to want total intimacy.

Kate stood up from the table and tossed the cold tea from her cup into the sink. She turned on the taps and watched the liquid dilute itself and disappear down the drain as if it had never been.

'I'll just have to make myself forget him,' she whispered tragically to the empty room.

But even as she said the words she knew she couldn't. Gerard Hunter would remain in her heart for as long as it continued to beat.

CHAPTER SIX

BRISBANE loved Christmas!

And it dressed for the occasion. The Queen Street Mall was decked out in all its finery. Enormous bells, floating angels, beaming Santas and dancing impish elves flitted, floated or rang through the sub-tropical city. Carols pealed out from almost every shop and buskers stood on street corners merrily competing in the general goodwill. Shoppers flocked into King George Square to view with awe the gigantic Christmas tree laden with decorations and lights which quite defied the imagination. It was a time of peace, a time to be happy and merry, a time to spend with loved ones.

And Kate was caught up in this spirit the way she was every year. She just couldn't help it. It was part of her nature to be happy, and her biggest joy was in seeing others happy. It acted like a tonic on her and was far more effective than any drug. Besides, Gerard had rung her at home after her first day back at work!

She had returned to her flat after an exhausting day of reporting with the desire to do little more than prepare a light meal, have a hot bath

101

and go to bed. When the telephone rang she thought it would concern the segment they had filmed which had caused some turmoil. A sexist group wanted Santa Claus to shave his beard!

But it wasn't the manager of the television studio. Kate would recognise Gerard's deep voice anywhere, and her face lit up with instant pleasure while her heart pounded with new hope.

'Do you usually work this late?' he growled into the telephone. 'I've been trying to reach you since five-thirty.'

'You have?' she asked breathlessly. 'Is everything all right? How's Matthew and——'

'Where have you *been* till this hour?' he cut in.

'At work. I've only just got home.'

'At work! Until this hour? It's eight o'clock!'

Kate smiled at his tone. He was concerned about her and she loved him for it.

'Uh-huh, and I'm exhausted.'

'Well, I don't like it, Kate.' She pictured the dark frown on his face as she listened to it in his voice.

'It's not so bad,' she confessed softly, knowing that if she was with him she would be removing that frown with her lips. 'How is Matthew?'

'He's fine.' Tiredness crept into his voice. 'He misses you.'

Kate chewed her bottom lip. 'I miss you

both!' she said in a voice so low she felt Gerard couldn't have heard.

But he had. She could almost see him dragging his hand through his hair and when he spoke his voice was gruff. 'It's hell here without you, Kate. I can't believe you've only been gone a few days.'

She wanted to ask, 'Do you miss me?' but instead she said, 'I'll be home at Christmas.' She had said *home*.

'I . . . Matthew can't wait that long.' A heavy pause. 'We're flying down to Brisbane on Wednesday. If there's time, perhaps we could get together for lunch?'

Her heart thumped wildly. She hadn't expected to hear from him, let alone *see* him before Christmas.

'I'd like that. Where should I meet you?'

'I'll pick you up from work. I know the place. Would one o'clock suit?'

'That will be perfect,' she agreed happily.

'Good. Now here's Matt. It was his idea we phone you.'

Matthew's idea or Gerard's, it really didn't matter to Kate. It was enough that he had called. After all, he must have *liked* Matthew's idea or he wouldn't have rung.

Matthew's childish voice bubbled across the wire and brought a fresh smile to her face.

'Hi, Kate. Guess what?'

'Hi, ol' Matt, what?'

'Mr Kit-Kat comes *here* to *our* place for his snack.'

Kate's grin became a chuckle. 'Why, that old so-and-so!' she exclaimed, 'I can't say I'm surprised, I could tell Mr Kit-Kat was taking quite a shine to you.'

'I think he *loves* me, Kate.'

Kate heard the almost desperate need in Matthew's voice and she had to swallow hard before answering.

'I know he does, Matt,' she answered softly. 'Now, you take good care of yourself because old Mr Kit-Kat isn't the only one who loves you. I do too.'

'And I love you, Kate,' he answered promptly, happily. 'Good night.' Strange clicking sounds came over the wire, followed again by Matthew's voice. 'Did you get those, Kate? They were kisses!'

And then there was only the sound of the dialling tone against her ear. Kate hung up and walked dreamily around her flat. Her men had called and she would be seeing them soon. She counted the hours.

She was waiting in front of the television studio when Gerard pulled up in a gleaming silver-grey Rolls-Royce at precisely one o'clock on Wednesday afternoon. He got out of the car and walked towards her, looking magnificent in an expertly tailored grey suit and crisp white shirt. Despite the heat of the day he appeared cool and relaxed. He greeted her with a warm smile, his eyes sweeping appreciatively over the pale silk dress which gave a sophisticated elegance to her slender figure, while the pastel shade of green brought out the deeper green in her eyes.

'Kate,' he said, taking both her hands in his and gazing deeply into her eyes. Kate's heart somersaulted in her chest. She wasn't aware of the curious glances nor the looks of admiration from her colleagues as they shuffled past them. Her world was in front of her in the person of Gerard Hunter.

'Gerard,' she murmured softly, while a thrill of excitement swept up her arm and all the way to her heart as he tightened his grip on her hand and led her to the waiting car.

It wasn't until Gerard was walking around to the driver's side that Kate realised Matthew wasn't there. Gerard climbed in beside her, his long legs stretching out with plenty of room in the spacious interior while his eyes caught and held her own. Suddenly a dangerous glitter appeared in the deep blue.

'Do you always wear dresses like that to work?' he asked accusingly.

A delighted smile danced across Kate's lips. 'Always,' she teased.

Black brows drew together in a dark frown. 'Isn't it a bit much?'

'Don't you like it?'

'I love it!'

Her fine brows arched enquiringly. 'Well, then?'

Gerard leaned towards her and cupped the side of her face with his large hand. 'Oh, Kate,' he said huskily, his thumb running lightly across her mouth. 'You just don't realise the effect you have on men.'

Abruptly he drew away and started the car steering it from the kerb and away from the studio. He glanced in the rear-view mirror. 'Curious mob, those.' He shot Kate a sharp glance. 'Have you been out with any of those fellows?'

She hunched her dainty shoulders in a shrug. 'A few,' she admitted casually, enjoying herself. She considered it a good sign that Gerard was displaying the green eye of jealousy.

His hands tightened on the steering wheel and Kate smiled a secret smile. 'Anyone in particular?' he growled. 'Anyone you especially like?'

'Not at the studio,' she answered mysteriously. His eyes gleamed down at her and her temperature rose dramatically. 'We're mostly just friends.'

Gerard's hands relaxed on the wheel and he sighed. 'That's good.' He smiled down at her upturned face. 'I really do love that dress!'

Kate chuckled and relaxed against the soft

leather upholstery, grateful for the air-conditioning which fanned her warm cheeks. The winding road down from Mount Coot-tha where the studios were located stretched in front of them, the dappled sunlight from the stately trees splashing across the bonnet of the car and against the windscreen. She could imagine the whisperings going on at the studio and knew she would be bombarded with questions when she returned. Who was that tall, dark, handsome stranger? She knew people would ask, and she couldn't really blame them. After all, she would be curious too if one of the other girls had been picked up by someone with Gerard's imposing good looks, not to mention this car!

'Where is Matthew? Are we going to pick him up somewhere?' Her face was turned to his, her eyes devouring the handsome profile.

'He's at Bargara.'

Kate's eyes widened. 'Bargara?'

Gerard glanced at her and chuckled. 'He's staying with Mrs Abbott for a few days.'

'At her *farm*?'

'Mm.'

Kate poked his arm. 'Come on, tell me, don't be such a tease!'

Gerard laughed. 'Two of Mrs Abbott's bantam hens have hatched some chicks. Need I say more?'

'I suppose not,' she grinned happily. 'Isn't

it wonderful, the change in Matt? It wasn't so long ago that he wouldn't even speak to Mrs Abbott.' She sighed happily. 'He'll have a wonderful time at the farm.'

'Yes, and it was good of her to offer,' Gerard agreed. 'I have to be here for a few days and didn't know what to do with him. I have an apartment here but couldn't leave him for most of the day while I attended to business. On the other hand I couldn't expect Mrs Abbott to forsake her farm day and night for our sake . . .' He glanced down at Kate and sighed. 'Being a single parent isn't all that easy, you know,' and Kate smiled at his expression while she made a daring suggestion.

'Perhaps you won't always be a single parent. Who knows, you might decide to marry again.'

'Not very likely!'

Now it was Kate's turn to sigh. She dearly wished he hadn't been so adamant in his statement.

They pulled up to a fashionable restaurant which Kate had heard about but never experienced. The men she dated were mostly from the studio and their salaries were on a par with her own—adequate but not substantial. Gerard handed the doorman the keys and then guided Kate into the dimly lit interior where a table for two had already been booked. The head waiter called Gerard by name, as had the doorman, and Kate heard the deep respect in their voices. Gerard was obviously well known here and it seemed they couldn't do enough to please him.

'Everything is ready, Mr Hunter,' the head waiter beamed down at them after they were seated. From the shadows an ice bucket containing a bottle of chilled white wine was produced and poured into their glasses, while avocados filled with fresh prawns were placed in front of them.

Gerard grinned at Kate's astonishment. 'I took the liberty of ordering for us when I made the booking. Hope you don't mind?'

'Well, no, I . . .' She looked down at the food on her plate. Several times at the beach she had made lunch for herself and Gerard and this was what she had served because both had admitted to having an insatiable appetite for avocado and prawns. Her eyes rose slowly to meet his and her breath caught in her throat. The small space separating them seemed charged with electricity, sparking the magic which had driven them so many times into each other's arms.

The burning flame of desire smouldered in his blue eyes. Her heart soared at the sight of it as his gaze swept longingly over her. A fierce tension gripped them. 'Your lunch hour will soon be over,' he said almost crossly, breaking the spell. 'Better eat.'

Kate picked up her fork but she couldn't

eat. Her pulses were racing and her senses were reeling. She marvelled that Gerard could sit so calmly as though nothing had happened, as though he had felt nothing while she knew with certainty that he had. She had seen it in his face, in his eyes. How could he just sit there and eat!

Achingly she watched him, her gaze studying the strong jaw and deep cleft, the firm line of his mouth, the wide brow framed by thick black hair, the laugh lines at the corners of his eyes which crinkled when he laughed, the deep blue colour of his eyes with those extraordinarily long lashes. A wistful sigh escaped her lips. He was so aggressively male and virile that her whole body throbbed in response to his nearness.

He looked up and saw her watching him. 'Eat up, Kate.'

'I can't.'

'Why not? Don't tell me you're not hungry, because I know you too well for that. You're always hungry, especially when it comes to your favourite foods.'

Green flecks shimmered in her very wide eyes as she stared helplessly across at him. A heavy silence fell between them, gripping the air with an unbearable tension. Kate dragged her eyes away and stared miserably down at her plate. She was torturing herself by loving him. There was no future in it. He had already admitted he would never remarry.

She should get up and walk out. She should never see him again. She should go somewhere else for her holidays. She should . . .

'Kate?' Gerard's gentle voice broke into her wild thoughts and she lifted her eyes to his face. Slowly he reached across the table and covered her hands with his.

'Is something wrong? Aren't you feeling well?' She squeezed her eyes shut at the concern in his voice.

'Kate?' he continued to probe gently. 'Should I take you home?'

With great difficulty she managed to draw herself together. 'No, I'm fine.' She forced a smile. 'Hey, look at that! You've finished yours while I haven't even started.' Avoiding his eyes, she picked up her fork and began eating, not stopping until every morsel was consumed. She hadn't tasted a thing.

'That was delicious,' she announced, dabbing daintily at her lips with her napkin while Gerard watched on, blue eyes filled with puzzled amusement.

'There's more to come,' he drawled, just in time for their plates to be removed and replaced by others. Kate stared in horror at the dazzling array of seafood. Again her favourites, and she knew she would be expected to eat. Gerard had ordered to please her, but it wasn't food she needed from him.

'How lovely,' she said weakly, and then did her best, explaining that she usually didn't eat much for lunch because it made her sleepy while at work.

'Well, that won't happen today,' he drawled. 'Your rosellas eat more than you do!'

Dessert came, a pavlova topped with swirls of whipped cream and mountains of fresh tropical fruit. It was a work of art. It was also her favourite dessert. But she knew she couldn't possibly eat it. Her stomach heaved at the sight of it and she looked at him with sheer terror in her eyes.

'Gerard!' she exclaimed weakly. 'Oh, Gerard, I think . . . I think I'm going to be *sick!*'

He was by her side in a flash, pressing her head down and applying a napkin wrapped around ice from the wine bucket to her forehead and temples. Almost instantly she felt better. The waiters hurried over, anxiously enquiring if everything was all right, wringing their hands in despair as other diners turned their way before looking dubiously down at their food.

Gerard paid their bill, and assured the owner of the lovely little restaurant that the young lady had been working too hard and had rushed through her meal in order to get back to her job. 'The food was excellent as usual,' he finished by saying, as he steered poor Kate out of the restaurant and into the dazzling sunshine.

'I'm sorry,' she murmured weakly as he helped her into the car. 'That must have been very embarrassing for you,' she added after he had slid in beside her.

Gerard turned in his seat and quietly studied her. Her long slender neck rose like the stem of a flower from her lovely shoulders. Her face was very pale and her lips were trembling. The soft hazel eyes were partially hidden by their fringe of silky gold-tipped lashes. Suddenly she bowed her head and her shoulders shook. Gerard reached for her instantly, cradling her in his strong arms.

'What is it, Kate?' he murmured against her hair.

Kate shook her head and tried to push him away, but his arms tightened around her. 'You've been working far too hard,' he scolded. 'I'm taking you home.'

'N-no.' She straightened in his arms and looked up at him. His eyes were dark with concern. 'I . . . I'll be all right. It was just as I said, I'm not used to eating so much in the middle of the day.'

He clearly didn't believe her. His gaze slipped over her face, stopping at her eyes which she quickly lowered lest he correctly read the message printed there directly from her heart.

'Very well,' he replied curtly, moving away from her to start the car. Neither spoke as they drove up the mountain to the studio. Kate felt heavy with despair. She blamed herself for spoiling their luncheon. She had allowed her feelings to get in the way of their relationship; a relationship which meant nothing more to Gerard than what he obviously took it for. They were friends. Nothing more, nothing less. She had been the buffer between himself and his son, and for this he was grateful.

'You said you would be in Brisbane for a few days,' said Kate as they stood in front of the studio.

'Yes, that's right,' Gerard agreed, his eyes riveted to the top of her head where the sun caught and lit every strand of her hair, transforming it into a shimmering fiery halo about her small face.

Kate swallowed her pride. 'Will I be seeing you again?'

He kept his eyes on her hair for an instant longer before dropping them to her face. 'Would that be a good idea?' he asked, pinning her with his glance.

Kate shifted uneasily, lowering her eyes. What did he mean, as if she didn't know? Would she *swoon* again? Pink touched her cheeks, highlighting their paleness.

'I don't know. It's up to you.' She moistened her lips with the tip of her tongue and forced herself to meet his penetrating gaze. His eyes were so dark today, she found herself thinking, losing herself in their glittering depths.

He reached out and touched a lock of her hair, curling the silken threads around his finger. His hand brushed her cheek.

'Of course you'll be seeing me again,' he said almost harshly, dropping his hand and stuffing both into his pockets. 'How else will I know if you're taking proper care of yourself?'

A happy smile touched her lips. 'Tonight?' she asked hopefully.

'You're a little witch, do you know that, Kate?' he sighed. 'All right, tonight, I know where you live. I'll pick you up at eight.' With that, he pivoted sharply and got in the car, and Kate watched until he drove out of sight. She glanced at her watch.

'Eight o'clock,' she said aloud. 'That means I only have six hours to wait!'

CHAPTER SEVEN

As Kate had suspected, she was bombarded with questions as soon as she entered the studio. However, she was reluctant to disclose much about herself and Gerard other than she had met him while she was holidaying at Bargara Beach. It was while she was talking and attempting to work at the same time that the peculiar feeling she had had during lunch returned, making her feel quite weak and not just a little sick.

'What is it, Kate?' someone asked. 'You look a little green.'

'Thanks,' Kate replied weakly, attempting to laugh which failed dismally. 'Green is my favourite col . . .'

And then she fainted, falling in slow motion to the floor while her friends looked on in horrified amazement. The next twenty minutes or so became a blur. Kate felt the softness of pillows behind her head, the cool of an ice-pack on her forehead and finally the voice of the sister in the infirmary.

'How are you feeling now, Kate?' she was asked by the middle-aged woman in a crisp white uniform.

'Much better, thank you, Sister,' Kate replied weakly, gingerly touching her throbbing temples. 'I must have fainted.'

'You did indeed.' The sister regarded her through narrowed eyes. 'Ever fainted before?'

Kate shook her head and then winced. She had never had a headache quite like this before either.

'It could be the heat,' the sister mused. 'Then again, it could be a virus. Better check with your doctor.'

'I will,' Kate agreed weakly, just as a telephone rang. It was for her.

'Kate Chalmers speaking,' Kate said into the mouthpiece.

'Kate!' Gerard's voice exploded into her ear. 'What's wrong?'

'N-nothing,' she replied, conscious of the sister nearby.

'*Nothing?* What do you mean, *nothing?* I was put through to several different departments before someone finally said you were in the infirmary!'

Kate did some quick thinking. If she told Gerard she was ill he would call off their date tonight. On the other hand she couldn't risk another fainting spell, especially after she had made such a fool of herself at the restaurant.

'With my job it's not unusual to be racing around to all the various departments,' she explained quickly, 'although I must admit it must be tedious for anyone trying to reach me.'

She heard a sigh of relief. 'When I was told you were in the infirmary, I thought you must be ill, and I blamed myself for not taking you straight home after lunch.'

Kate hated lying to him but if she was to see him tonight she had to continue. Besides, she was feeling much better.

'I'm fine, Gerard, really.' She lowered her voice, speaking softly into the mouthpiece. 'Why did you ring?'

'I was worried about you,' he growled. 'I wanted to find out how you were. You didn't look well when I left you.'

Kate smiled and closed her eyes. He was worried about her, he cared! When she opened them again, the dizziness returned and she had to fight the rising nausea in her stomach. She clutched tightly on to the telephone, feeling the perspiration on her palms.

'Gerard, instead of going out tonight how about having dinner at my place?'

'Fine.' A pause. 'Kate, are you sure you're all right? You sound rather strange.'

She *felt* strange! 'I . . . I really must go now, Gerard. See you tonight, only make it six o'clock,' she added with a false gaiety. 'Dinner won't wait.'

She hung up and pressed her fingertips to her temples while every bone in her body decided to ache at precisely the same instant. The sister looked at her pityingly and shook her head.

'You've got yourself a humdinger of a virus, young lady, and the best thing you can do now is to go home and get into bed.' She stuck a thermometer into Kate's mouth, and reached for her wrist to take her pulse. 'Better ring that young man back and cancel your date. You won't be able to make yourself a cup of tea, let alone prepare a meal!'

Despite offers to drive her home, Kate stubbornly drove herself home, weaving her way slowly but steadily through the traffic and stopping at a shopping centre to buy the necessary items for the meal she planned to cook for Gerard. No miserable virus was going to keep her from whipping up something special for the man she loved despite the gloomy forecast from the sister at the infirmary.

By the time she got home with her purchases she was almost too weak to stand. She swallowed some aspirin and went into her bedroom to change.

She gazed longingly at the bed, every aching bone and muscle begging her to lie down, to have a little rest. The clock on the bedside table told her Gerard was not due for almost two hours. She gave in to temptation and stretched sideways on to the bed. Just for a few minutes she told herself, before she fell into a heavy sleep.

Somewhere deep in her subconscious she

thought she heard the shrill sound of a bell ringing. It seemed to go on and on for ever and then blessedly it stopped, only to be replaced by a thumping, banging sound. Kate moaned in her sleep and dreamed that someone was hitting her head with a sledgehammer. She crawled across the bed, small whimpering sounds gurgling from her swollen throat as she tried to escape the pounding blows. Suddenly the room was flooded with a brilliant light and she sat up in bed, gazing bewilderedly about the room, her eyes glazed with fever.

'Kate!' Gerard rushed over to her. 'Good heavens, Kate . . .' He knelt beside her on the bed, smoothing back the damp tendrils of hair from her fever-flushed cheeks. 'So you really are sick,' he said slowly. 'Why didn't you tell me when I rang you at work?' he chastised her gently as he gathered her into his arms and cradled her against his chest. 'All that ruse over being in different departments . . .'

'Oh, Gerard,' Kate whimpered against his chest. 'I feel so awful, I really do. I think I'm going to *die!*'

He pressed his lips against her brow. 'You're burning up, but you won't die,' he soothed her, smiling into her unnaturally bright eyes. 'Come on, let's see if we can get your temperature down and then I'm calling a doctor.'

He scooped her into his arms and found the bathroom, setting her down carefully while he fiddled with the shower taps to find the right temperature before turning to help her off with her clothes.

'This is no time for modesty, Kate,' he growled as she protested weakly, making a feeble effort to hide her nakedness from him.

He was right, she certainly was in no state to object, and she couldn't have managed the shower without his help. He had shrugged out of his jacket and rolled up the sleeves of his shirt, supporting her while the cool waters washed over her, effectively reducing her temperature.

'How do you feel now?' he asked huskily as he squeezed the water from her hair and wrapped a towel around her body.

'Much better, Gerard,' Kate sighed as she snuggled against him, feeling his pounding heart against her cheek. 'You've been so kind, I'll never forget it.'

'What are friends for?' he asked drily, setting her away from him while he held on to her shoulders. She felt his fingers dig into her flesh. 'If you weren't so sick I'd give you a good thrashing for lying to me this afternoon!' He gave her a little shake. 'Why did you *do* it?'

Kate rang her tongue nervously over her lips. 'I thought you wouldn't come if you knew I was s-sick.'

'Why the hell not?' She shrank from the anger in his voice.

'Well, I don't know,' she admitted miserably. 'It's just what I thought, that's all.'

His face darkened. 'You little fool!' He pulled her roughly to him, his arms tightening around her as he picked her up and held her close to him. 'Now,' and his eyes glittered their warning, 'I'm going to put you to bed and then I'm going to call the doctor. Count yourself lucky that I'm such a patient man!'

'Yes, Gerard,' Kate answered meekly, completely subdued by that kiss.

He carried her into the bedroom and set her down on the bed. 'Now where do you keep your nightgowns?' he asked, then not waiting for an answer found them on his own, slipping a white cotton nightdress carefully over her head.

'Now, hop in,' he ordered, pulling back the single blanket and pink sheet, and carefully smoothing the latter over her after she had stretched out. He had loosened his tie and undone the top buttons of his shirt, and she saw his shirt was quite damp where she must have splashed him during her shower and felt oddly guilty about this. Tears sprang to her eyes and rolled down her cheeks.

'Now what?' asked Gerard.

Kate looked up at him through her tears. 'I feel so miserable,' she admitted.

He sighed and sat down beside her, taking her hand and holding it. 'That's understandable,' he soothed. 'You'll feel brighter when you're feeling better.'

'But I invited you for dinner,' she continued plaintively, fresh tears flowing down her cheeks. 'You should be eating by now . . .'

'Sssh,' he whispered softly, stroking her hair from her forehead. 'I'm not hungry.'

'But it's not f-fair,' she sniffed. 'I wanted to have everything so n-nice for you, but instead . . .'

'But instead you're ill and feeling rather sorry for yourself,' Gerard interrupted. He patted her hand and tucked it under the sheet, rising to his feet. 'I'll ring the doctor now.' He smiled down at her. 'Stop blaming yourself. Everyone's ill now and then.' He turned to leave.

'Gerard?'

'Yes?' he sighed.

'Are we really just friends?'

His face darkened. 'What kind of question is that? Of course we're friends!'

'But *just* friends?'

His eyes narrowed on her flushed face. 'Don't knock friendship, Kate, it might be all some of us ever have.'

Kate was hardly aware of the doctor examining her or of the sharp prick in her arm. Dimly she heard Gerard's deep voice as he consulted with the doctor and then all was quiet as the injection started to take effect. The room was in darkness and Gerard became a darker shadow as he remained sitting on the side of the bed, his hand cool against her fevered brow.

Gradually he stretched out beside her. In her sleep she turned towards him, nestling against his long, lean length. Gerard slipped his arm under her, pulling her head on to his chest. Kate sighed in her sleep and it was a sound of deep contentment. Gerard smiled down on her, his fingers stroking her hair while the moonlight shone through the opened windows framing them both in a heavenly glow.

When Kate awoke in the morning it was with a feeling of wellbeing. She was nestled in the crook of Gerard's arm while one of her own arms was stretched across his chest, her hand inside his shirt. She lay for several minutes, not moving lest she wake him before she had had her fill of watching him while he slept. His beard had grown during the night, giving a blue-black haze to the already dark complexion. Long, spiky lashes splashed against his cheeks and his hair was an unruly black mass across the pillow-slip.

Her eyes slipped down to his chest and she saw that his shirt buttons had been completely undone! Colour filled her cheeks. Had *she* done that? Her fingers caressed the silky black hairs sweeping across the tanned muscular expanse, toying their way down to the waistband of his slacks and finally resting on the buckle of his belt. A delicious excitement filled her, complementing the wonderfully warm feeling of security and contentment that lying beside him gave her. If only he loved her, how gloriously happy she would be.

Gerard stirred in his sleep and Kate held her breath lest he wake. She didn't want him to! She wanted to keep him here for ever. When he awoke she knew he would leave her to go and attend to the business which had brought him to Brisbane. His hand came down and covered hers and she looked up to catch his lazy smile.

'Trying to seduce me in my sleep, Kate?' he asked with wicked glints in his eyes. For a split second she didn't understand what he meant, not until the hand covering hers pressed gently and she became aware of the buckle under the palm of her hand. She tried to snatch her hand away, but he held it firmly and she became conscious of the sudden stillness in the room as an electrifying tension gripped them both.

'I . . . no . . . of course not!' He removed his hand and she got shakily out of bed, holding back tears of disappointment that he should so easily let her go. Grabbing her robe from the bottom of the bed, she walked proudly from the room, grateful for the long nightdress which covered her shaking knees.

Once inside the bathroom, she leaned against the door staying there until her breathing became normal. She ran a shaky hand through her hair as a deep feeling of weakness washed

over her reminding her of how ill she had been
the night before.

Slowly she undressed and stepped under the
running shower. Her hair didn't need it, but
she shampooed it anyway, wanting to take as
much time as possible to give Gerard time to
get out of her flat and, if she was lucky, out of
her life! *Oh, no, she didn't really mean that!*

The shower door slid open and through the
suds falling from her hair, Kate blinked up at
Gerard. He was naked except for a bright green
towel tied around his waist. He gave her a
rueful grin before having the audacity to
enquire if there was room for him. Kate spun
around without answering, turning her back to
his question and to himself. When she heard
the shower door closing she congratulated
herself on being so firm. It was high time she
stood up to the great Gerard Hunter, letting
him realise he couldn't mess around with *her*
feelings. If he rang her during the remainder
of his stay in Brisbane she would be coolly
polite towards him but *nothing else*. She
certainly wouldn't agree to any dates and . . .

She felt his presence too late! Also she was at
an obvious disadvantage, what with her hands
raised to her head as she furiously worked the
suds into her tingling scalp. Gerard's hands slid
around her slender waist, pulling her towards
him. Kate gasped. Her eyes had been squeezed
tightly shut against the sudsy stream of water,

but now they flew open, with cruel results.

He reached for the shower nozzle and directed it straight on to her, rinsing the suds from her hair before gathering her close and kissing her hard. Kate responded with a passion which matched his own.

Gerard trembled against her, his steely arms bending her to his will, his mouth leaving hers to burn a fiery trail across her jaw.

'Kate!' he groaned. 'This is insane!' He raised his head to look at her, saw the love in her eyes, the fever burning in her cheeks. His eyes filled with a wretched misery as he suddenly grabbed her close, burying his face in her throat. 'Kate!' and it was as if her name was torn from the depths of his tortured soul.

Instantly, Kate stiffened, her desire rapidly fading as once again he set her away from him, a shadow masking the deep blue of his eyes while he ran a rueful hand through the dark wetness of his hair. Without a word she stepped from the shower, wrapped herself in a towel and ran to her bedroom, where she threw herself on to the bed and lay huddled in a cloak of misery.

Gerard took his time in following. She listened to the sound of the water running and knew he was calmly continuing his shower. Using *her* hot water, *her* soap and probably her shampoo and—yes, when he sauntered into the bedroom she saw he had taken a fresh towel from *her* linen closet. Never mind that she was wrapped in the green towel he had worn into the bathroom. It wasn't that she didn't want him using her things; in fact she liked the feeling of intimacy this sharing gave her. What hurt was simply this: he didn't want *her*.

'Get out of that wet towel,' he growled as soon as he saw her shivering on the bed.

Kate muttered something unintelligible and snuggled deeper into the cold, wet towel. She would probably catch pneumonia and die, she thought miserably, when suddenly the towel was snatched away and she was forced by very strong hands to stand on her feet. She glowered up at him while he made no effort to conceal his impatience. Just as he had done the night before, he got her into a fresh nightdress and warm dressing-gown. She refused to look at him, riveting her eyes to the silky black hairs splayed across his naked chest.

'How do you feel today?' he asked gently, and she couldn't believe he was asking her this almost as if he had forgotten what had happened in the shower. She felt a moment of panic as hysteria rose in her throat.

'How do I feel?' she shrieked. 'As if I'm going to *die!* Do you hear me, Gerard Hunter?' she continued shrilly, her hands pummelling his bare chest. 'That's how I feel and it's your fault!'

He grabbed her hands and swung them behind her, holding them with one of his own while his other cupped her face. An angry flush was evident on the hard planes of his cheeks as he looked down at the fiery green daggers flashing in her eyes. His hand slipped behind her head and his mouth came down hard on her own. She fought to resist him, but in vain as he continued to plunder the sweet interior moistness, punishing her for her outburst and perhaps something more, far more.

When he finally let her go, Kate sank on to the edge of the bed, raising her hand to her mouth weakly.

'You . . . you beast!' she whispered, eyes wide in a very pale face as she looked up at him.

'Let that be a lesson to you,' Gerard ground out the words. 'I haven't time for tantrums.'

'T-tantrums?' She might have overstepped her mark with him, but he had set her aside once too often. She had to know why.

'I love you, Gerard,' she said softly. 'You must know that. How can . . . how can you just turn *away* from me?' She looked appealingly up at him, tears shimmering in her beautiful eyes. Gerard clenched his hands and unclenched them as a small muscle hammered alongside his jaw.

'You don't know what you're talking about, Kate,' he said raggedly, and the naked misery in his eyes tore at her heart. She reached for his hand and pressed it against her cheek.

'Oh, Gerard,' she whispered brokenly. 'Don't you realise you're just like Matthew was before . . . before he let out his hurt?' Tears sparkled like jewels on her silky lashes. 'I love you, Gerard, you must see I do.'

She wasn't prepared for the bitter laugh that sprang from his throat. 'Love?' he spat out the word as if it had a vile taste. 'Love belongs in the movies or in romantic novels—it doesn't belong *here!*' and he slammed his fist against his chest. 'If it's love you want, Kate, then look for someone else. You won't find it with me!'

If he had struck her it would have been far kinder. His words tore at her, breaking her, knocking the wind from her lungs and settling like a knife in the pit of her stomach, twisting, turning, edging upwards to her heart, threshing it into a million pieces. Her cheeks lost their colour, her lips paled and her eyes became dark hollows in her head.

Without another word, Gerard got dressed while Kate watched, believing she was sitting on the edge of the worst nightmare of her life. With his jacket slung over one broad shoulder he stood in front of her. She hadn't moved.

'You'll be all right?' he asked quietly.

Kate didn't look at him. She couldn't. All she wanted now was to be left alone with her broken heart.

'Kate?' He knelt in front of her, taking her cold hands into the warmth of his. 'Kate, I'm sorry, I shouldn't have been so hard on you, but . . .' He drew her hands upward to press them against his forehead. She could feel the thick unruly hair against her skin. She dragged her eyes up to his face and saw that his eyes were closed, the black brows drawn tightly above them. Was it possible that he was hurting as much as she was? Kate wondered while she ached to hold him in her arms.

The telephone rang, brutally interrupting their stillness, perhaps destroying whatever chance they had to begin a new understanding. It rang several more times before Gerard rose to his feet, pulling Kate up with him. He followed her into the lounge and picked the phone up for her, their hands touching as she took it from him.

While she spoke, Gerard busied himself in the kitchen boiling water for coffee and preparing soft-boiled eggs for her breakfast. Several minutes later, Kate stood just inside the kitchen door, her hand on the frame for support. Gerard looked up and frowned immediately.

'What is it, Kate? Not bad news, I hope?'

She was amazed to hear herself laughing. 'That was my father ringing from Western Australia. Business is bad, in fact it's terrible. He and my brother need capital. You'll be glad to hear he wants to sell the cottage.' Tears streamed down her cheeks. 'Isn't that wonderful news, Gerard?' she sobbed. 'You won't have to put up with me being your neighbour any longer!'

CHAPTER EIGHT

GERARD made Kate eat the soft-boiled eggs he had prepared for her and drink the coffee he poured into her cup.

After she had eaten he placed a tablet in the palm of her hand. The doctor had left them the night before and Gerard told her they were to be taken after meals. She was to have today and tomorrow off work and use the weekend for the rest of her recovery. According to the doctor and Gerard she would be fine by Monday.

But Kate knew something that they didn't. She would never be 'fine' again. Gerard had thrown her out of his heart, not that she was sure she had ever been there in the first place, and her father would be selling the dear little cottage at Bargara, her only link to Gerard and the place she had loved since childhood. Fate had dealt her a double blow. She bowed her head while she allowed herself the luxury of a few minutes of self-pity, savouring it, before firmly casting it aside.

She picked up her breakfast dishes and carried them to the sink. 'I wish you'd have some breakfast too, Gerard,' she said as she tilted her head back to look up at him.

'Coffee will do for now,' he answered in a tone which wasn't nearly as pleasant as her own. 'I'm catching a flight to Melbourne and will have breakfast on the plane.'

Kate stiffened. 'Melbourne?'

Gerard nodded and put his coffee cup on the draining board alongside her dishes. 'Yes.' He glanced at his watch. 'I'll barely have time to change before I head for the airport.'

Kate's throat felt dry. 'I didn't realise you'd planned on going to Melbourne.'

'I hadn't *planned* on it,' he said moodily, 'but circumstances have arisen which require my attention.'

'With Ria, or your business?' The words rolled off Kate's tongue before she even realised she was thinking them. 'I'm sorry,' she sighed. 'I . . . I had no business asking you that.'

'That's right,' he told her coldly. 'But since you did you may as well have your answer.' He straightened and took in a deep breath. 'Most of my time will be spent on business, and I might drop in on Ria. Does that satisfy your curiosity?' he added cruelly.

Anger flared within her at his coldly mocking tone.

'Not in the least!' she snapped back, her eyes flashing. 'I fail to understand why you'd want to see Ria after she has caused you and your son so much pain.'

'And I fail to understand why you should think it's any of your business!' Gerard snarled back.

His words chilled her. Hadn't she already confessed her love to the man? Hadn't she witnessed Matthew's heartache and been on the receiving end of Gerard's bitterness? Of course Ria was her business. Wasn't it Ria who stood between them now? Suddenly Kate realised she held Ria personally responsible for Gerard not loving her!

'Gerard, please, I have to know,' Kate whispered, her eyes searching his for the truth, 'do you still love Ria?'

His eyes fastened on to hers, holding them with a blinding light. 'She *is* the mother of my son, after all.'

Kate could feel herself shrinking under Gerard's penetrating gaze. 'Yes, yes, I know, but does that give her licence over you for . . . for ever?'

The light faded from his eyes. He looked tired and much older than his thirty-four years. 'Yes, it does!'

Kate felt numb. The sink was behind her and she leaned against it. There was still one question he hadn't answered, and she had to know the truth.

Summoning all her willpower, she pushed herself away from the sink and squared her small shoulders, her eyes fixed bravely on his.

'Gerard,' she said softly, 'I know Matthew will always be the bond between you and Ria, and I can accept that.' She took a deep breath. 'I've tried not to love you, but I can't help myself. Once the cottage is sold, we'll probably never see each other again unless——' Kate gazed helplessly up at him, but it became evident that he wasn't going to help her. 'Gerard, please tell me. Are you still in love with your ex-wife?' She couldn't bring herself to say the woman's name.

The silence which followed was ear-shattering. Kate's heart was thumping so loudly she felt certain Gerard could hear it. Her eyes never wavered from his face, but it was impossible to tell what he was thinking. Like so many times in the past, his features were carefully masked.

'Gerard?' she prompted gently.

His shoulders slumped and he stuffed his hands into his pockets. 'Let it drop, Kate,' he sighed. 'I have neither the time nor the inclination to discuss my former wife with you, or with anyone else for that matter.' He brushed past her towards the door. 'The only thing you should be concerned with is getting better.'

Kate rushed after him. 'I wasn't after a *discussion*,' she hit out angrily, grabbing his arm. 'A simple yes or no would do!'

He glanced pointedly down at the small slender hand on his arm, but she made no effort to remove it. If anything she had the desire to dig her nails into his, to hurt him, to . . .

His gaze went slowly to her flashing eyes and then down again to her hand. A harsh grin spread across his ruggedly handsome features. 'Feeling the urge to scratch my eyes out, Kate?' he asked softly, his tone taunting.

Instinctively her hand left his arm and she slapped him hard on the cheek, stinging her palm. Horrified by her action, she stood trembling in front of him, wildly wondering why he hadn't stopped her. Already she could see the mark of her hand on his cheek and she felt deeply ashamed.

'Now that you've got that out of your system,' he said softly, his eyes raking her face, 'perhaps you'd like to kiss me goodbye!'

Kate's eyes widened in dismay. 'Kiss you?' she gasped, feeling the urge to strike him again. '*Never!*'

He shrugged and turned towards the door.

'Wait!'

Gerard slowly turned, his smile cruelly mocking her.

'I thought you'd change your mind,' he growled, while tears of outrage flooded her eyes. Kate angrily brushed them aside, her body trembling with fury.

'Why must you be so insufferably arrogant?' she lashed out at him. 'How can you be so cruel?'

The mocking smile deepened, carving dimples into his hard cheeks. 'And why must you poke that cute little nose into areas it doesn't belong?' he returned icily, raven-black brows arched over deep, blue eyes. 'Now kiss me.'

Kate's heart was skipping erratically all over her chest as the enigmatic light in his eyes held her captive.

'Gerard,' she whispered achingly, her mouth trembling. 'Please, Gerard, don't——'

A hardness crept into his eyes while a pulse beat frantically alongside his jaw. 'Kate.' Her name was drawn out warningly and she dared not refuse. She stepped closer and raised her mouth to his, standing on tiptoe. He made no effort to help her.

'Put your arms around me,' he commanded, and she put her hands on his chest, working them slowly up to his neck, and then her arms were around him, her body pressed to his.

'Kiss me!' he groaned, and his voice was hoarse.

Kate touched his mouth with hers. Her body trembled, betraying her urgent need for him. His eyes gleamed down at her, knowing what this was costing her.

'You can do better than that,' he commanded, his tone lightly caressing. 'You said you love me. I want to *feel* it in your kiss!'

Kate dropped her arms and pressed her hands against his chest. She didn't deserve this humiliation, she *didn't!* Gerard's arms closed around her, pinning her against his male hardness, hurting her. He *wanted* to hurt her, this she knew.

'Gerard!' she gasped. 'Let me go!'

He held her at arm's length for several seconds before swiftly drawing her against him, kissing her savagely, while his hands roamed freely over her body, her muffled cries falling on deaf ears. When he finally released her, her body was on fire.

'Now tell me you love me!' he commanded harshly. 'Tell me!'

Tears welled in her eyes as she stared silently up at him. The fiery anger died in his eyes, replaced with bleak despair. Slowly his hand slipped from her head and fell to his side.

'Kate,' he groaned, 'did we ever have to meet?' When Kate didn't answer he sighed. 'You're right,' he agreed tautly, 'that question doesn't deserve an answer.'

'Perhaps it does,' Kate whispered tearfully. 'Perhaps we were meant to meet.'

He studied her in silence for several long seconds while she stood quietly in front of him looking small and fragile in her bathrobe. Fresh pain filled his dark eyes. 'But not to love. It's no use, Kate,' he declared thickly. 'I've hurt enough people in my life. I don't want to hurt you.' He turned towards the door. 'I'll ring you from Melbourne to see how you are.'

After he had gone, Kate wandered aimlessly around her flat. She felt exhausted, but when she lay down it only seemed to increase her restlessness. Finally she dragged herself out of bed and got dressed. She spent the day in the park, a pale lonely figure wandering through the gardens and resting under purple-flowering orchid trees, while it seemed all around her young couples in love strolled by, holding hands or with their arms wrapped around each other. Their love had brought them happiness, while the love she had for Gerard was one-sided and doomed not to expand. He would never love her—she knew that now. His broken marriage had taught him something Kate didn't know how to change. It had taught him not to trust in love or marriage.

By nightfall Kate returned to her flat. Friends popped in after work but left soon after when they saw how sick she was. She didn't tell them what was really wrong with her. How can you explain a broken heart? The television was turned on for company and she found herself watching one of Matthew's favourite programmes, remembering the times the three of them had munched popcorn from a communal bowl while they sat in front of the set, laughing, Gerard's arms around her and Matthew on his lap.

Kate switched off the television and walked over to the telephone. She picked it up and dialled Mrs Abbott's number. When she heard dear old Abbey's voice she felt peacefully reassured. There was still some warmth left in her world. They talked for several minutes before the telephone was handed over to Matthew, and Kate smiled at the eagerly happy voice coming to her over the wire.

'Guess what, Kate? Daddy called just before you did. He called all the way from *Melbourne* and now you're calling all the way from *Brisbane*!'

We're all so far away from one another, Kate thought, woefully, connected only by a fragile coil of wire. She swallowed convulsively and tightened her grip on the phone.

'Did you get those cards I sent you?' she asked, forcing a cheery note into her voice.

'I sure did, and I loved them!' Matthew exclaimed, before bursting into a fit of giggles. 'I loved the drawing too, of me feeding the rosellas. You do draw funny, Kate.'

Kate chuckled, feeling better now than she had the whole day. Matthew's happiness was contagious and she gave in to the joy of just listening to his voice.

'What about old Mr Kit-Kat?' she asked, still chuckling. 'Did I do him justice or not?'

Fresh laughter tumbled through the wire and into her lonely ear. 'Was *that* old Mr Kit-Kat?' Matthew squealed with childish glee. 'Abbey and I thought it must be one of her old roosters!'

'Hey, that's not fair. I put a lot of time into that drawing,' protested Kate, grinning from ear to ear. 'I thought he looked a real treat.'

Matthew's whoops of laughter trickled right down to her toes and she joined in as they remembered her clumsy attempts at art. When the laughter finally subsided Matthew's voice became suddenly wistful.

'I miss you, Kate. I wish Christmas would get here so you can come home.'

Pain tore at her heart. Home. The cottage. Soon there would be neither. Poor little Matthew! How was she ever going to tell him that after Christmas they might never see each other again? She knew he had come to love and trust her. He was just a child, a baby. He would never understand that she had to leave, that there was no place in his home for her, just as there wouldn't be in the cottage after it was sold. God help us all, she thought as tears sprang to her eyes. We're victims of love, the three of us—Matt, Gerard and myself. *What about Ria?* A voice inside her screamed. Suddenly Kate understood. Ria had the key which held them prisoners. Until Ria relinquished that key, Gerard would never feel free

to love Kate the way she knew he wanted to.
He was a man of honour, of deep pride, and it
was this honour and pride which made him
feel personally responsible for the failure of his
marriage. He blamed himself, and he would
go on blaming himself until eventually he was
destroyed.

'Kate? Katie? Are you there?' Matthew's
anxious voice broke into her thoughts.

'Yes, yes, of course I am, darling.'

'I thought you'd gone without saying
goodbye,' he said tearfully.

'I would never do that, Matthew,' Kate said
gently.

'Well, you didn't hear what I said,' he came
back accusingly. 'I said I love you.'

How young he sounded and oh, how very,
very vulnerable!

'I heard you, and I'm glad, because I love
you too, sweetie. So very, very much.'

'And you'll be home soon?' he continued
anxiously.

'You bet I will!'

But there was something she had to do first.
Early the next morning Kate was on a flight
heading for Melbourne. In her handbag was
the address of the Boyntons, given to her by
Mrs Abbott after Kate had finished speaking
with Matthew. Surprisingly, Mrs Abbott
hadn't questioned her about why she wanted
the address.

Kate leaned back and closed her eyes. She was tired, having had next to no sleep the night before. Gerard had rung her just after she had hung up the phone from speaking with Matthew and Mrs Abbott. A half-smile formed on her lips as she remembered their conversation.

'Kate? I've been trying to reach you the whole day. Where in blazes have you been?'

'I went to the park.'

'The *park?*' his voice had exploded over the phone.

'Yes, I felt restless and I needed to think.'

A heavy silence drifted through the wires before Gerard spoke. 'You went to the park to *think* when you're just over a virus?'

'Yes.' She had taken a deep breath. 'I always go to the park when I'm . . .'

'Troubled?' He had supplied the word for her and she had nodded into the phone. Gerard accepted her silence and understood. 'Oh, Kate!' he had groaned, and she knew he was clutching the telehone just as tightly as she was. 'What have I done to you? To us?'

'We might have a chance yet, Gerard,' she whispered, while tears stung her eyes. She had rushed on, 'When will you be leaving Melbourne?'

He was a while in answering. 'I'm holding a conference first thing in the morning and flying out before lunch.'

He would be gone from Melbourne before her plane landed. There wouldn't be even the slightest chance of running into him while she was there. The success of her plan depended on his absence. Kate knew Gerard would never allow her to visit his ex-wife.

'Kate?' Her name had been followed by a tortured sigh. 'I'll be going straight to Bargara Beach. I . . . I won't be stopping in Brisbane.'

No! Was this his way of saying goodbye? 'I see,' Kate had whispered achingly.

Another heavy silence. When he spoke again Kate could barely recognise his voice. 'Take care of yourself . . . my darling!'

Then he hung up, and Kate had sat holding the phone for a long time before she finally replaced it on the receiver. No matter what the outcome of her meeting with Ria, Kate knew Gerard's last two words would remain with her for ever. *My darling!*

She shivered in protest against the air-conditioning which she was certain was turned up full. The male passenger sitting next to her smiled down at her pale face. Kate didn't notice the smile nor the way the young blond man edged closer until his shoulder was touching hers.

'Not very talkative, are you?' he enquired smoothly, and Kate raised startled hazel eyes to the smiling face.

'No,' she muttered, edging away from him

to view the clear blue sky which held not a trace of cloud. The plane was circling over Sydney and the passengers were treated to a breathtaking view of the coast leading up to the Sydney Harbour Bridge and the spectacular Opera House. The sparkling blue waters churned under the activities of small speed-boats darting out of the paths of hydrofoils and huge lumbering ferries, their decks crowded with people.

The sun blazed down on graceful skyscrapers which speared the blue skies. There were plenty of parks, and it seemed to Kate that every tree was in blossom while rolling green lawns gave way to masses of flower beds which provided a sea of shimmering colour. The pilot spoke and she obeyed the order to fasten her seat-belt.

There would be a one-hour wait before her connecting flight to Melbourne. She refused an invitation from the young man to have a drink in one of the many airport lounges, and when he shrugged and walked away Kate silently wished him better luck on his next trip.

Kate spent the hour anxiously waiting for it to pass! She hadn't been able to eat the break-fast served on the plane, and while she felt hungry she couldn't swallow the raisin toast she had ordered in the cafeteria, although she did manage three cups of coffee. The hot liquid helped relieve the pain in her throat which was fast becoming swollen. She wished she had remembered to bring the tablets the doctor had prescribed, and despite the comfortable temperature in the cafeteria she felt cold and shivery. The virus had a good grip on her now.

Kate dozed on and off during the flight to Melbourne. The passenger sitting next to her, this time an elderly woman, had to wake her up to tell her they were landing and to fasten her seat-belt. She managed this with shaky fingers before drifting again into a dreamless world only to be awakened by the stewardess informing her they had landed.

Melbourne was suffering from a heatwave, and after stepping from the air-conditioned plane on to the tarmac Kate felt she had entered a furnace. By the time she had walked the distance to the terminal her blue skirt and lighter blue blouse were clinging to her. She could feel the perspiration running down her back.

She managed to get a taxi almost immediately, instructing the driver to take her to a hotel she had stayed at with her parents the few times they had visited Melbourne. Kate knew it to be fashionable, respectable and, above all, reasonably priced. She couldn't afford to be too extravagant. Her air fare had taken a big chunk from her savings as it was.

It was with no small amount of relief that she finally found herself in the comfortable quarters of her hotel room. The first thing she did was to remove her notebook from her shoulder bag and dial the Boynton residence. The telephone rang several times before it was finally answered, allowing Kate plenty of time to build up her anxieties. It hadn't occured to her that the Boyntons might not be at home.

Enid Boynton sounded pleasant and had been expecting her call. Abbey, bless her heart, had rung earlier, thereby paving the way for Kate. Kate accepted an invitation for afternoon tea at four o' clock. After she hung up, she remained sitting on the edge of the double bed for several minutes before getting up to shower and dress for the occasion.

The occasion.

Kate was never able to forget the next twenty-four hours of her life.

CHAPTER NINE

'So Gerard doesn't know you're here?'

Kate sipped at the iced tea Mrs Boynton had poured into her glass and shook her head.

'No,' she answered, carefully placing the glass on the small wicker table which separated them.

'Then I don't think we should be discussing him.'

Kate leaned forward. 'I haven't come all this way merely to gossip! Please, Mrs Boynton,' she pleaded, 'you've got to help me. I must know about Ria!'

'But why?'

'Because she hurt Gerard and Matthew. She hurt them badly. I . . . I love them, Mrs Boynton, but——'

Mrs Boynton's eyes narrowed shrewdly on Kate's flushed face. 'Does Gerard love you?' she asked quietly.

Kate hesitated. 'Yes, I think he does.'

Mrs Boynton arched her brows. 'You *think* he does?'

'Yes,' Kate answered simply, and Mrs Boynton saw that love in her beautiful hazel eyes. She was silent for several minutes as she studied the quiet determination on Kate's face, and Kate knew she was considering just what she would say and how much she would reveal.

'Gerard was a young geology student when he first met Ria,' Mrs Boynton slowly began. 'Ria was studying art at the same university. Her family had a great deal of money, while Gerard had to take on part-time work to keep himself at the university.' Mrs Boynton shrugged. 'They fell in love and got married.'

Kate sighed. 'I had already guessed that,' she said softly. 'What happened after they were married?'

Mrs Boynton chuckled. 'You're really determined to drag all that I know from me, aren't you?' she asked, and then at the look on Kate's face, became suddenly serious. 'Very well, then, if it does any good I'll be glad. I'm sure any information I give you will be treated sensibly, and I believe you when you say you love Gerard *and* Matthew. They're both very special people,' she added quietly, 'and I have a feeling that you must be special to them.' She reached across the small table and patted Kate's hand. 'Where should I begin?' she mused aloud.

'After their marriage,' Kate prompted gently.

'Yes—well, as I've mentioned, Ria's family had money and, as they were obviously taken with their new son-in-law, wanted to help

Gerard in his business. Gerard refused help, and that's when the trouble began. He was determined to make it on his own, while Ria was equally determined not to do without any of the creature comforts she had grown up with. Gerard had started his oil-drilling exercises and Ria spent money faster than he could make it. He was away for long periods at a time, and when he was home she made life unbearable for him. They'd decided on a divorce when Ria discovered she was pregnant. Naturally Gerard called the divorce off.'

'Did they try to make a go of things after that?' asked Kate, thinking of the joy the prospect of a baby would bring.

Mrs Boynton smiled sadly. 'No, if anything the situation became worse. Ria became very bitter. She didn't want the child and wanted to have an abortion.'

'No!' Kate gasped.

'I'm afraid so, and she would have succeeded if Gerard hadn't become suspicious. He got to the clinic just in time to stop her.' Mrs Boynton brightened and smiled. 'Isn't Matthew a lovely child?'

'He certainly is,' Kate agreed, chilled by the knowledge that he might never have been. 'He's so much like Gerard.'

'A perfect replica,' Mrs Boynton nodded.

Kate sat back in her chair and pressed her fingers to her throbbing temples. 'What was

Ria like as a mother?' she dared to ask. 'Matthew was very upset when they first moved to Bargara Beach. Perhaps Abbey told you the trouble we had with him. He refused to talk to anyone.'

Tears filled Kate's eyes. 'He and Gerard just seemed so . . . so *alone!*'

Sympathy flooded Mrs Boynton's eyes at Kate's obvious distress. 'You must remember what they'd both been through,' she gently reminded Kate. 'But they're not alone any longer, are they, dear? They have you now!'

'Oh, Mrs Boynton,' she sighed wistfully, 'if it was only that simple! I don't think Gerard will ever risk marriage again.'

'But you said he loves you.'

'Yes, I believe he does.'

'And you obviously love him.'

'Yes, I do.'

'Have you told him how you feel?'

'Yes,' Kate sighed, 'I have.'

Mrs Boynton's brows shot up. 'And?'

'He told me——' Kate cleared her throat with great difficulty, 'he told me to look for love with someone else.'

Mrs Boynton chuckled and Kate looked up in surprise.

'Dear Kate,' the older woman said, 'never listen to what a man *says!* Listen to what his heart tells you. You said you believe he loves you. You've been listening to his heart.'

I *have* been listening to his heart, Kate thought as she gazed across the spectacular landscaped gardens towards the swimming-pool. The three Boynton children, all in their teens, had arrived home from school and were having great fun in the pool. There was love and understanding in this home, and Kate had no doubt that Mrs Boynton was responsible for most of it. She had made their house a home and she was without doubt the centre of her family's security. She was, quite simply, the children's mother, her husband's wife. The world would always seem a better place for them because they had learned to trust it from the very beginning.

Kate turned back to Mrs Boynton and smiled. 'You've taught me a great deal today,' she said. 'Thank you.'

Mrs Boynton responded by passing Kate a tray of sandwiches and refilling her glass. 'If I've been of any help I'm glad,' she said when she had settled back into her chair. 'However, I'm certain you would have come to all the right conclusions on your own. You strike me as a sensible girl.' Her eyes twinkled. 'Sensible *and* beautiful. Gerard is a very lucky young man.'

Soft colour flooded Kate's cheeks as she turned once again to watch the children in the pool. They were conducting races now and there was much laughing and cheering.

'Would you consider it sensible if I paid Ria a visit?' Kate asked softly as she continued to watch the children.

'I would not!' Mrs Boynton responded vehemently.

Kate turned sharply. 'But why?'

'Because there would be nothing gained,' Mrs Boynton answered simply.

'But she was Gerard's *wife!*' Kate responded, anguish showing plainly in her eyes.

'Yes, she was, Kate, and that's a fact you'll never be able to change.' Mrs Boynton leaned forward. 'Ria belongs in the past. If you're sensible you'll keep her there,' she added shrewdly.

Kate knew Mrs Boynton was right. There was nothing to be gained, and Ria did belong to the past. Still——

'She may no longer be Gerard's wife, but she'll always be Matthew's mother.' Kate's voice broke.

Mrs Boynton sighed and shook her head. 'Ria used her child just like she used everything in her life. She was never actually a mother to him, not in the way you or I would use the term. Nannies took care of the boy when Gerard was away on business, and you must remember, Kate, Gerard and Ria haven't lived under the same roof for years. The divorce was merely a formality.'

'But Matthew was so upset when Gerard

took him from her,' Kate protested as she wrung her hands.

Mrs Boynton smiled sadly. 'Yes, I can imagine the act Ria would have put on but, believe me, it would have been to hurt Gerard. Ria wouldn't have cared what damage she did to the child.'

As Kate prepared to leave Mrs Boynton offered to drive her to the hotel, but Kate declined. 'I've taken up enough of your time,' she said, kissing the older woman's cheek.

'Time well spent, I hope,' Mrs Boynton responded smilingly. 'I have a feeling we'll be seeing more of you.'

Kate returned the smile but didn't answer. She knew she would never be truly satisfied until she faced the enemy, and Ria was still the enemy. She had caused grave damage to the two people Kate loved most in the whole world. She had to be certain Ria would never hurt any of them again. She took a deep breath and quietly asked Mrs Boynton for Ria's address. Mrs Boynton started to protest, but at the look in Kate's eyes sighed and gave it to her. Kate jotted it down in her little notebook and hurried to catch the waiting taxi.

She instructed the driver to let her out half a block before Ria's house. She paid the driver and walked slowly down the leafy tree-lined street. Dusk was fast approaching and the street lights were already on. The air felt hot and clammy and not a leaf stirred. Kate counted the numbers off as she passed each home. Ria's place was in the same exclusively wealthy district as the Boyntons' and the homes were old and well established. Despite the almost overbearing heat, Kate shivered when she finally found herself standing outside Ria's gate. She suppressed a powerful urge to smile when she read the signs prominently displayed on the wrought-iron enclosure: TRES-PASSERS WILL BE PROSECUTED and BEWARE OF THE DOG. From what she had learned about Ria the warnings seemed in character.

But they did nothing to boost Kate's self-confidence. She stood staring at the words while visions of herself being torn apart by ferocious dogs raced across her mind. Further up and almost obscured by the ensuing hedge was another sign: RING FOR GUARD. Below this was a round white button. Kate started to reach for it when suddenly the gates started to swing open. At the same time there was the distinctive sound of a car's motor. Kate darted to one side of the gate, pretending she was a passer-by as a long, low and very sleek red sports car zoomed between the parted gates and halted just outside them. A tall blonde woman stepped from the car and took the few steps necessary to reach the white button which shut the gates. Turning back to the car, she glanced at Kate, and Kate was struck by the cold, flat, blue eyes that flicked carelessly over her. The woman's brows were highly arched, giving the long, rather thin face a look of perpetual surprise. Kate was about to speak when another voice sounded from the car. It was far from pleasant.

'Hurry up, Ria. Do you want us to miss the opening number?'

Despite the warmth of the evening Ria wore a mink wrap. She turned up the collar as she hurried to get back into the car. Kate caught a glimpse of a fat, balding man wedged behind the steering wheel, his pudgy fingers adorned with gold rings.

'Darling, don't be such a grouch!' Ria admonished laughingly. 'Did you notice that waif beside the gates? A most unusual-looking creature. I had the feeling she wanted to speak to me for some reason.'

The car roared off, drowning Ria's words. Kate watched until the vehicle was out of sight. Sighing heavily, she turned and walked back down the street. She hadn't spoken to Ria, but now she knew it was no longer necessary. Ria's cold blue eyes had told her all she needed to know.

Kate stepped from the kerb and there was a screeching of brakes. A tall, lean man jumped from the shuddering vehicle and grabbed Kate's arm.

'You little fool!' a familiar voice bellowed into her astonished face. 'Are you trying to kill yourself?'

'*Gerard!*' Kate gasped, and her eyes flooded with spontaneous delight as she gazed up at his scowling features. 'Oh, Gerard, I can't believe it. It's *you*! It's really you!'

The dark blue eyes softened, but only for a split second before they hardened. 'I can't believe it's me either,' he ground out sarcastically. 'I must be a fool to come tearing after you like this!' His grip tightened on her arm as he drew her closer. 'You have a lot of explaining to do, and it had better be good!' Without a further word he thrust Kate none too gently into the front seat of a pale blue Volvo estate. Sliding in beside her, he reached over and cupped her chin forcing her to look at him. There were tears sparkling in her eyes.

'Kate, Kate,' he declared huskily, shaking his head in despair as he wiped the tears from her cheeks. 'Stop that now, do you hear?' he begged as the tears continued to flow unabashedly down her fever-flushed cheeks. He pressed the back of his hand to her brow and frowned. 'You're burning up!' He drew her close and kissed her, his lips gentle as they followed the path of the tears. 'What am I going to do with you?' he groaned as he cuddled her against his chest. Kate closed her eyes and a tiny sigh escaped her lips. He smelt so good, like cinnamon-flavoured toffee apples and aftershave. His heart beat a soothing tattoo against her cheek. She wished she could stay in his arms for ever listening to his voice murmuring against her hair as he quietly scolded her. She reached up and lightly ran her fingers across his jaw, tracing the deep cleft in his chin. He took her hand in his and kissed each pink-tipped finger. His eyes were closed.

A sharp rap on the window made them both start. They looked and saw a young policeman gazing curiously in at them. Gerard rolled down his window.

'Yes, constable?'

'I would like to point out, sir,' the young policeman said shyly, 'you're parked illegally.'

'Thank you,' said Gerard. 'I was merely helping a lady in distress.' He rolled up the window and grinned at Kate while he started the car's motor. Kate grinned back at him.

'Imagine!' she said teasingly. 'A lady in distress.'

'You will be once I get you back to your hotel room,' Gerard answered, the laughter leaving his eyes. 'And this time, no more tears! They're too damned distracting!' He glanced sharply down at her. 'You have a lot of explaining to do.'

'Can't it wait until tomorrow?' Kate pleaded. 'I'm still not feeling well, you know. Remember my virus?' she cautioned wisely.

'Cut it out, Kate,' Gerard ground out warningly. 'If I didn't know how sick you are I would have turned you over my knee back at the kerb and given you a sound spanking!' Blue eyes glittered down at her. 'That's exactly what I felt like doing when I learned you were in Melbourne.'

Kate nervously ran her tongue over her lips. 'I have a right to go where I please,' she dared say.

Gerard snorted angrily. 'You apparently think you have the right to do just about anything you please. Now be quiet,' he snapped as she started to protest, 'anything you say now will only make the situation worse!'

Kate drew herself up stiffly. 'I was only going to tell you which hotel I'm staying at. It's the——'

'I know where you're staying,' he said harshly. 'I happen to know every move you've made since you so foolishly left Brisbane.'

She frowned at him suspiciously. 'How could you know? Do you have spies working for you?' Her voice rose indignantly. 'I have a right——'

'Say that one more time, Kate, and so help me you'll be sorry.' His voice was ominiously low and Kate wisely swallowed the rest of her sentence. Better to let him concentrate on the traffic, she decided as she turned her attention to the fabulous Christmas decorations lining the streets while the strains of Christmas carols

filtered through the car windows. She felt
Gerard relax beside her, saw the whiteness
disappear from his knuckles as he gripped the
wheel. She realised he mistook her silence for
meek obedience. What he didn't realise was
she was saving her strength for the battle he
threatened would soon be under way!

Gerard parked the smooth-running Volvo in
the hotel car park and then escorted Kate up
to her room. He took the key from her hand
and inserted it in the lock, pushing the door
open while he gripped her elbow. She heard
the door slam behind them and realised he
must have kicked it shut. He was working
himself into a real temper and she shivered
involuntarily.

The room seemed cold and harsh under the
glare of the ceiling light. She snatched her arm
from Gerard's grasp and went over to switch
on the table lamps. Gerard smiled coldly as he
in turn switched off the overhead light. The
room instantly looked better, warmer and far
cosier. Only Gerard's glacial smile as he pinned
Kate with his eyes caused the chill she felt in
her heart.

She sighed and looked down at the pale
yellow frock she was wearing. She felt messy
and longed for a bath. As if reading her mind,
Gerard suggested she take one. She looked up
gratefully while a half-smile formed uncertainly
on her lips.

'You're sure you won't mind?'

He shrugged. 'Why should I?' He loosened his navy blue tie and unbuttoned the neck of his shirt before stretching out on the bed and closing his eyes. A moment later he opened one lid and peered at her.

'What's wrong?'

'N-nothing,' Kate answered a little breathlessly.

'Well then, why aren't you in there taking your bath?' he enquired reasonably.

'I . . . I was just wondering what you were going to do?'

'This!' he announced lazily, folding his arms under his dark head and shutting his eyes once more.

'Well, for goodness sake!' snapped Kate. 'Don't you dare fall asleep!'

'Mmm, I might.'

'What about our *fight*?'

'I'm resting for it!'

'What if you fall asleep and wake up only to find me gone?' she wailed.

'Then I'll just have to find you all over again, won't I?' His eyes half opened as he peered at her through hooded lids. 'And *that* would really make me angry!'

Kate fumed quietly as she gathered her things and prepared for her bath. He was playing with her, toying with her feelings, threatening her one minute, practically scaring her out of her wits and then having the nerve to lie down and sleep! She walked over to the bed and stood staring down at him.

It didn't seem right that one man should be blessed with so many attributes. Those lashes alone! What woman wouldn't crave them? On any other man they might look feminine, but not on Gerard. They only enhanced his masculinity, a striking contrast to the hard, rugged planes of his face, the smooth hardness of his jaw. His lips were slightly parted revealing the brilliance of white teeth against the darkness of his skin. Kate bent her head and lightly kissed his cheek. If he was still asleep by the time she had finished her bath she would pluck one of his eyelashes and tickle him awake!

She enjoyed the luxury of a long hot bath. It had been a hard day, but she felt the trip had been worth while. At last she knew what sort of life Gerard had lived over the past several years. She could understand his bitterness, his reluctance to love again. And just as importantly she no longer felt threatened by Ria. Ria belonged in Gerard's past. Kate longed to be part of his future. She would fight for him . . .

Fight! Would they have a quarrel? she wondered as she stepped from her bath and dried herself with a fluffy white towel. She certainly hoped not. Maybe the rest Gerard was having would put him in a better frame of mind. He had looked tired, exhausted in fact. She wondered why he hadn't left Melbourne as he had planned. Something must have happened with his business preventing him returning to Bargara Beach. Kate slipped into a white skirt with matching white top. It was the outfit she had planned on wearing home tomorrow. She brushed her hair until it shone and applied a light touch of lip-gloss to her full mouth. Her throat felt much better and the aches and pains had all but left her body. The virus was working its way out of her system.

It was a feeling of wellbeing that Kate had when she stepped from the bathroom. Gerard's eyelashes were safe. He was up and standing by the window peering out at Melbourne's nightlife. Kate hesitated. His rigid stance seemed threatening somehow and she realised with a sudden sinking of heart that he really did intend to question her about her day. She would have told him all about it. *Some day!* When she had digested all the facts, got used to what she had learned, when she didn't feel quite so emotional about everything.

He half turned, sensing her presence, and his eyes swept appreciatively over her slender body before returning to her face. He still looked tired. He couldn't have slept and Kate felt guilty about the time she had spent in the bathroom. He had obviously been waiting for her. He shoved his hands into his trouser pockets.

'How do you feel?'

'Much better, thank you,' Kate replied in a strained voice. She became aware of a tension developing between them which was far from friendly.

He nodded curtly. 'You look better. Not so flushed.'

'It must have been one of those twenty-four hour things,' Kate murmured, watching him closely. His eyes seemed almost black and deep lines were drawn in his face.

'I ordered dinner.' He indicated with a slight turn of his head a table set for two and several domed-top serving dishes on a trolley beside it. 'I thought we would eat here.'

Kate swallowed hard. 'That was very considerate of you.'

A cynical smile twisted his lips. 'I thought so. We'll have privacy for our discussion.'

'Gerard, couldn't it wait?' she pleaded anxiously. 'You look so tired and I'm just getting over my virus. Neither one of us is up to a discussion.'

Her plea fell on deaf ears. 'We'll eat first, talk later.' He pulled out one of the two chairs for her.

'I'm really not very hungry, Gerard, and——'

'Sit!' The commanding voice cut her off and by the gleam in his eyes Kate knew she dared not refuse. She took her place at the table and spread a white linen napkin across her lap. Her hands were shaking.

The meal of fresh crab salad followed by chicken done in a creamy wine sauce was truly succulent. Gerard ate with hearty appetite and while Kate thought she wouldn't be able to eat a thing, she surprised herself by eating almost as much as he did.

'You must be better,' Gerard drawled approvingly as she ate the last of the crusty rolls and finished the wine in her glass. How many glasses had she had, she found herself wondering, knowing she had drunk plenty in an effort to boost her confidence, her bravado?

After they had finished their dessert of fresh strawberries and cream Gerard wheeled the trolley across the room and out of the door. Kate watched in breathless silence as he returned to her, taking her hand and leading her to the small two-seater sofa. The interrogation was about to begin! She shivered and peeped cautiously up at him through the silky fringe of her lashes. Their shoulders were touching and his thigh was pressed against hers in an exhilaratingly delicious contact.

He had been so attentive during their meal. Surely he wasn't going to spoil it all by being too hard on her now? But at the look in his eyes as he gazed down at her Kate wondered if she and Gerard had just shared their last supper!

CHAPTER TEN

SHE jumped up from the sofa. Her palms were damp with nervous perspiration and she dried them self-consciously on the sides of her white skirt. Her legs felt weak and her knees were shaking and she was aware of her pulse throbbing erratically.

Gerard's expression as he watched her was granite-hard. He spread his arms along the top of the sofa and stretched out his long legs. 'I realise you're a reporter, Kate, and I accept that reporters are experts at poking their noses into places they don't belong. However, I didn't think *you* would stoop so low as to go behind my back in an effort to check me out!'

His eyes flicked over her, whip-sharp, and the colour rose in her face at his accusing look.

'But I didn't,' Kate protested weakly, her voice quivering.

His black brows shot up sardonically, icy scorn in the glitter of his deep blue eyes. 'You didn't spend the better part of two hours with Enid Boynton?' he jeered.

'Well, yes, I did, but——'

'And what did you talk about? Melbourne's notorious weather?'

'Gerard, please——'

'*Gerard, please!*' he mimicked her tone. He slowly rose to his feet. 'Can you imagine what you've put me through?' he asked hoarsely. 'I was half out of my mind with worry! When I got to Brisbane and you weren't there——' He shook his head. 'No one knew where you'd gone. Your car was there, so I decided you must have walked to the park. I went looking for you. Finally, I rang Mrs Abbott thinking she might know something.'

Kate's heart filled with despair at the look of anguish in his eyes. It hadn't occurred to her that he would stop in Brisbane, he had *said* he wouldn't. *Listen to what a man's heart tells you, not to what he says!* Mrs Boynton was right, Kate acknowledged. Gerard cared for her, his previous actions had proved this. She should have trusted him and not given in to her wild desire to know what his life had once been.

'Oh, Gerard,' she whispered again, her voice breaking. 'I . . . I'm so s-sorry!'

'Sorry!' he rasped, the word exploding in the still room. 'Sorry for what? For sneaking behind my back? For prying information out of a trusted friend? For making me chase after you, wondering what in tarnation you were up to?' He shook her roughly. 'For all that?'

A deep hurt clung to her eyes as she met his tortured gaze. 'Yes, for all that,' she agreed quietly.

He was silent for several minutes, his eyes never leaving the exquisite beauty of her face. A nerve twitched in his jaw and her heart ached at his tired appearance. Her hands moved up his chest to the dark silky hairs showing through the opened collar of his crisp white shirt. She felt him tremble when she softly stroked the tanned column of his neck before tracing the strong jaw and full lips. Her fingers gently touched the tired lines around his eyes and she ached to kiss them away.

Gerard grabbed her hands and held them tightly against his chest. 'And what did Ria tell you?' His voice was low and edged with fury. 'Did she tell you what you wanted to hear?'

Kate quickly shook her head. 'I didn't speak to Ria.'

His eyes raked her face and his complexion darkened. 'Don't add lies to what you've already done, Kate,' he answered grimly, distaste showing in the dark centre of his eyes.

'I tell you, I didn't speak to Ria.'

'Are you forgetting where I picked you up?' he demanded angrily, his fingers closing on the soft flesh of her arms.

Colour flooded Kate's cheeks as she gazed helplessly up at him. 'I know you found me on Ria's street corner, but I didn't speak to her. She was——'

'You mean you came all the way to Melbourne, hounded poor Enid for Ria's

address, took a taxi there and then didn't speak
to her?' He snorted his disbelief.

'I *saw* her.'

Gerard drew in his breath and let it out
slowly. At the same time he released the
punishing grip he had on Kate's arms. 'So-
o, you *did* speak to her. Well,' he demanded
harshly, 'did she fill you in on all the gory
details?' His eyes blazed down at her. 'Did
she?'

Anger and resentment flared within Kate.
Gerard was being unreasonable, refusing to
believe her, not giving her the chance to
explain. He wanted to hear the worst.

'*Yes!*' she hissed.

'And did you believe her?'

'Every word,' Kate bit out.

Gerard's blue eyes narrowed. 'You're lying!'

She slumped her shoulders in defeat. 'What's
the use?' she sighed, her heart sick with
despair. 'You've accused me both ways.' She
took a deep breath before continuing. 'I did *see*
Ria. She got out of a car to shut the gates. We
looked at each other, that's all. I admit I went
there with the intent to speak to her, but after
seeing her I didn't feel there was any need.' She
spread her hands in a gesture of hopelessness.
'Believe it or not, Gerard. It's up to you.'

Gerard turned away from her and walked
towards the windows, his hands thrust deeply
in his pockets as he stared into the blackness.

Fighting back tears, Kate went over to him and laid her hand on his arm. He tensed and she immediately dropped it. He didn't want her touching him and her heart broke.

'Gerard,' she whispered his name in a plea of anguish.

He slowly turned and faced her. 'I think we've both said and done enough, Kate.' He shrugged his broad shoulders and then turned as if to leave. Kate panicked. If he left now she knew it would be for good. It was as he said. They had both said and done too much and each was hurting on account of it. But to part now would be fatal. The wounds were too raw, they would fester and never heal. There would be no chance of going back. Their love would be lost for ever. Gerard picked up his suit jacket and slung it over his shoulder and walked towards the door. Words tumbled from her mouth, but they were straight from her heart.

'Gerard, I know you're upset and I blame myself. I should never have come here, I realise that now, but at the time I thought—I *hoped* I was doing the right thing. I love you so much, Gerard, you and Matthew, and I wanted you to love *me!*' Tears streamed down her cheeks as she continued her confession. 'I've longed to hear you say you loved me, Gerard, and when you didn't I blamed Ria.' Her voice now was a hoarse whisper. 'I wanted to convince myself that I was better than Ria, that I could

love you better, that you could love *me* if only
you would give yourself a chance! Give *us* a
chance.'

The silence which followed her words
became unbearable. Kate wiped her wet cheeks
while her heavy lids told her her eyes were
swollen and probably an unsightly red. But
none of that seemed to matter any more. He
had seen her at her best and at her worst. He
had looked after her when she was sick and
saved her from drowning. He had teased her
and tormented her and they had laughed and
joked together. Each had carried the other to
dizzying heights of ecstasy, but only one had
given their heart. Kate was the loser here, and
she knew it.

She swallowed convulsively as she looked up
at him, trying desperately to find something in
his eyes which would give her some shred of
hope that all might not be lost. But the eyes
which met hers were cold and unfeeling and
shrivelled her very soul. She moved from the
door, straightened her shoulders and gathered
what remained of her pride.

'I'll be at Bargara over Christmas,' she said
in a small voice, not looking at him. 'Matthew
would be disappointed if I wasn't and . . .' she
took a deep breath before she could continue,
'. . . and the cottage has to be put on the
market.' Her voice broke and she squeezed her
eyes shut.

'Kate?'

'Yes?' she asked, almost fearfully.

'Look at me, Kate.'

She half turned towards him and was struck by the misery in his eyes which exactly matched her own.

'What is it, Gerard?' she asked quickly, a tiny spark of hope springing in her chest.

He took a step towards her and his arm was outstretched. 'I . . .' He shook his head sadly and dropped his arm, and Kate felt the physical pain as the hope died in her chest.

'It's all right, Gerard,' she said quietly. 'I understand.'

'No!' he cried raggedly. 'You can't possibly *understand!*' The word was torn from his throat in a bitter explosion.

'Oh, but I do,' Kate continued ruthlessly, facing the truth at last and daring to confront him with it. 'Matthew isn't the link connecting you with Ria. It's your own bitterness. You enjoy being tormented by her. You feel you failed as a husband and you're using your feelings to punish yourself.'

His eyes blazed with anger. 'You don't know what you're talking about!'

'I know *exactly* what I'm talking about and so do you!'

He stood in front of her, tall and big and handsome, and in his eyes was a look of shocked disbelief at her words. He had the assurance and complete self-confidence which comes with a born leader and it was these qualities which had helped him create his empire and take his place in the world. He wasn't used to failure and it had never occurred to him that he hadn't failed Ria as a husband but that she had failed him as a wife! His bitterness wasn't towards Ria; it was reserved exclusively for himself. Kate marched stiffly past him and opened the door.

'You'd better go now, Gerard,' she said quietly. 'It's late and I'm tired and I don't think there's anything left to say.'

He stood in the centre of the room staring across at her, his face dark with colour and giving the impression that if he lived to be a hundred he would never understand women, Kate in particular. 'How did it happen?' he drawled softly as he made his way towards her, leaning against the frame of the door she held open. 'I was to chastise *you*, remember?'

'I suppose I wasn't the one in need of it,' she answered simply, her soft hazel eyes tinged with a sad regret. 'Goodbye, Gerard.'

His blue eyes turned a steely grey, as he pushed away from the door. 'You really want me to leave?' he asked hoarsely.

Kate swallowed hard and nodded. She knew there was too much bitterness in Gerard's heart to leave room for her. If only she had realised this sooner she might have spared herself the torment of loving him and the heart-wrenching pain of having to say goodbye.

'Very well,' Gerard replied curtly, his eyes lingering on her trembling lips for just a moment before he walked out of her life. Kate softly shut the door and leaned against it, listening to the whirr of the elevator as it stopped and started again. When Kate flew out of Melbourne early the next morning she was faced with the tragic irony of it all. She need never have come to Melbourne. Gerard had held the key which had locked her from his heart, not Ria. 'Oh, Gerard,' she whispered to the clouds swirling past the window, 'you were my love and my enemy!'

The final days leading up to Christmas were busy ones for Kate. Last-minute shopping was completed, gifts were wrapped and time not spent at work was spent cleaning her small apartment. She drove herself relentlessly, keeping busy, always busy so there was no time to think. Despite her hectic schedule and ensuing exhaustion, sleep was always long in coming and she would toss and turn, tortured by her love for Gerard and the heady dreams which followed. Already weakened by the virus, she lost weight and dark smudges of purple appeared under her eyes. Her friends and colleagues at work were deeply concerned, but no amount of questioning could make Kate reveal what was wrong. How does one explain a broken heart? she would often think in bleak despair.

Her family rang from Western Australia and her loneliness increased. It would be the first Christmas they wouldn't share together, the distance separating them far too great.

'I've contacted the agent I want taking care of the sale of the cottage,' her father said over the phone. 'He reckons we'll get a good price for it the way property values have increased over the years. Seems southerners, particularly from Melbourne, are flocking to the north in droves and are willing to pay handsomely for land on the coastal beaches. Do what you can, pet, to get the best price. We all know how much the cottage means to you, and I wouldn't sell it if we didn't need the money.'

'I know, Dad, and don't worry about me. I was getting tired of looking after the place anyway,' she lied.

'You mean that?' her father asked with obvious relief. 'Perhaps the upkeep has been a burden, not only to us but you as well.'

'I'll have to start thinking about new places to spend my holidays,' Kate tried joking into the phone, but her voice was flat and dull, totally lacking in hilarity. 'When will the real estate agent be round?'

'Saturday around lunchtime. You'll be there?'

'Yes, I'll be driving up after breakfast.'

'Good girl. Let us know how it all turns out.'

'I will, Dad.'

'Merry Christmas, Kate.'

'Merry Christmas,' she replied bravely, her voice as empty as her heart.

Always before the drive to Bargara Beach had been a happy event for Kate, filled with joyous expectation of long, sun-filled days spent on the beach and in the surf, and the evenings curled up in her favourite chair reading the many books she had brought along which she had stored in Brisbane and never found time to read. The sale of the cottage would put an end to all that and her heart was in mourning. By the time Christmas was over there would be nothing left. She had already lost Gerard and now the cottage was to be taken away from her as well.

The first thing Kate saw when she drove into the driveway and parked her car was the little white fence she and Gerard and Matthew had built. She walked slowly over to it and when she touched the smoothly painted surface the garden seemed to fill with the rollicking sounds they had made while constructing it. It seemed impossible now that they had had so much fun, had laughed so loudly and played such fun tricks on each other. Her eyes drifted over to the sweeping poinciana tree and colour touched her pale cheeks at the memory of passionate

moments under its velvety green branches and
scarlet flowers. She turned slowly around, her
soft hazel eyes not missing a thing. The garden
had never looked more beautiful and her poor
heart swelled with pride of what her grandparents and herself had achieved.

They had *created* this! This magic garden of
fairytale beauty where humming-birds drank
from dainty yellow flower cups and kooka-
burras laughed at the sight of rosellas and king
parrots nibbling greedily on the red berries of
the umbrella trees. One didn't have to search
the skies for a rainbow. It was right here in
Kate's garden.

Deliberately, Kate ignored Gerard's home,
but as she removed her suitcase from the boot
of the car her eyes were drawn irresistibly to
the imposing structure. Was he at home? Had
he heard her drive in or had the roar of the sea
blotted out the sound? Would he come over,
and if he did, what would they say to each
other? She caught her bottom lip between her
teeth and bit hard. Some sort of pretence would
be needed for Matthew's sake, and Kate wasn't
very good at acting. Poor little Matthew, she
thought sadly. He was bound to sense the
hostility between his father and herself and
experience a feeling of *déjà vu*.

She unlocked the door and placed her suitcase and parcels on the kitchen floor. Tears
stung her eyes. It didn't seem possible that

after so many years she would never see this place again. The new owners would undoubtedly knock it down and build something new and flashy.

The cottage was small but it was big on memories and each room held its own. Even the worn-out carpet had its story to tell. Tiny feet and big feet had set their mark there. Kate began removing pictures from the faded old walls, putting them in neat stacks along the floor. Grandmother's knick-knacks were carefully wrapped in tissue and placed alongside the pictures. She would have to do something about the furniture, arrange a moving van. There wasn't much and she really didn't know what she would do with it, but one thing was for sure. She wouldn't leave it here where it would undoubtedly end up in the tip or a second-hand furniture shop. Perhaps she would find a bigger place to live where she could include Grandmother's things with her own. Yes, that's what she would do, she thought as she tenderly stroked the worn old pieces while tears ran unnoticed down her cheeks.

Suddenly there was a hand beside her own. The hand was huge and deeply tanned, and her breath caught in her throat at the sight of it. Slowly the hand moved nearer her own and then it was on top of it, the long fingers entwining through hers. The huge tanned hand lifted the small pale one and her eyes lifted with it all the way up to Gerard's lips.

Their eyes met over their hands and each saw how the other had suffered. Gerard's face was haggard and there was pain in his eyes. His pale beige shirt hung loosely on his shoulders and his skin, usually so dark, was now the same faded hue as his shirt.

Kate's pretty pink floral sundress was a rude mockery to herself. There were no blossoms in her cheeks nor sunshine in her eyes. Both had been completely robbed of their vitality.

'You've lost weight,' Gerard said almost accusingly, 'and you look so pale!'

'I've been working hard,' she answered, and neither realised they were whispering. 'How is Matthew?'

'He's fine. He's been waiting for you.'

Kate tried to smile but found her mouth seemed incapable of the exercise. 'I . . .' she cleared her throat, 'I rather expected to find him in my garden.'

'He knows you're here. I wouldn't let him come over.'

Kate nodded and dropped her eyes. 'I suppose it's best,' she said tearfully. 'Was he very upset when you told him about the cottage being sold?'

'Yes, at first.'

She closed her eyes. 'I told you children were remarkable little creatures. After a while I suppose he won't even remember my name.'

'He'll *never* forget your name, Kate,' Gerard declared huskily.

He was still holding her hand and as she tried to pull it loose he held it tighter. She looked up at him with tear-filled eyes.

'Why did you come over, Gerard?' she asked, while tears glistened like tiny jewels on her lashes and finally rolled down her cheeks. 'Was it to hurt me some more?'

A cry of anguish ripped from his throat and through her own tears she saw his eyes were unnaturally bright.

'*Kate!*' He dropped her hand and she saw a tremor rip through his body. 'Kate, can't you *see?* I don't want to hurt you! I want to *love* you!'

'You want to love me but you *can't?*' Her voice shook. 'I've offered my love to you so many times, Gerard,' she continued sadly, 'but each time you've turned me away.' Somehow she found the courage to continue. 'I'm not going to let you do that to me again.'

'Kate,' he groaned, reaching for her, but she sidestepped him, knowing if he touched her then all would be lost. She couldn't get on that merry-go-round again. She had loved and lost. The brass ring had been there, but it had been impossible to reach. Somehow, somewhere, she would pick up the fragile threads of her life and learn to live again. It would be hard, but she would do it. She *had* to!

'We said our goodbyes in Melbourne, Gerard.'

This time there was no chance of escape as he lunged for her, grabbing her arms and jerking her almost savagely against the hard wall of his chest. '*You* said goodbye in Melbourne. I didn't!' He shook her. 'You said a lot of things in Melbourne and I listened carefully to each one of them, but I didn't listen to *that*!'

Kate stared up at him, hardly aware of the bruising pressure on her arms. It was his eyes which held her attention. There was a desperate quality in them she had never seen before. He was fighting for her, she could see that, and this knowledge filled her with wonder. She swallowed convulsively as she listened to his tortured voice.

'After I left you that night I walked the streets. Oh, I didn't go far, but I must have circled your hotel a million times. In the morning I bought some coffee and rolls from a pavement café and then I went up to your room.' His eyes blazed down into hers at the memory. 'You were gone! You'd already checked out.'

'I had no reason to stay.'

'Kate, don't be so cruel,' he groaned, wrapping his arms around her as he buried his face in her neck. He held her away from him so he

could look her full in the face. 'I went back
because I knew I couldn't live without you. I
went back to beg you to forgive me for being
such an insensitive fool. Oh, Kate,' he whispered brokenly, 'I went back to ask you to
marry me!'

'Marry you?' she asked breathlessly while
she was conscious of her heart skipping crazily
in her chest. 'Oh, Gerard!' Her eyes glowed.

'At first I refused to believe you'd gone.
When you didn't answer your door, I tried
breaking it down. I was almost arrested!' He
smiled ruefully. 'They took pity on me and let
me go after they showed me your empty room
and your signature on the register proving you
were no longer at the hotel.' He dragged his
hand roughly through his hair. 'I must have
just missed you.'

'Did you decide it was an omen? Is that
why you didn't come after me?' Her arms were
around him now. She wasn't even conscious of
putting them there. It just seemed the right
thing to do.

He smiled tenderly down at her, his eyes
devouring her face. 'My first thought was to go
after you, but then I decided I'd better cool
down first. I went to the park, just like you
once did.' His hands cupped her face, framing
her exquisite beauty in a tender circle of love.
'I did a lot more thinking there, my precious
darling, and I realised how empty my life had

been before I met you, and how bleak the future looked without you.'

She closed her eyes at his words and he bent and kissed her eyelids. 'Can you forgive me, my sweet, for not admitting sooner just how crazy I am about you?'

Kate opened her eyes and smiled up at him. 'Yes, I can forgive you,' she murmured softly.

He had been holding his breath, but at her forgiveness let it out slowly in a long sigh. 'And do you believe me when I say I've never loved any woman as much or as deeply as I love you?'

'Yes, I believe you,' she answered convincingly.

His arms tightened around her. 'Oh, Kate,' he groaned, 'I don't know what I would have done if you had said you didn't!'

Her hands went up to his face and she softly stroked the lines around his eyes, her fingertips brushing his lashes and smoothing his brows. 'I used to wonder what it would take to remove the chill I so often saw in your eyes,' she whispered lovingly. 'That chill is gone, Gerard,' she said, her voice filled with wonder. 'It's truly gone!'

His eyes shone down at her, filled with warmth and love. 'Perhaps it was fear you saw,' he said huskily, and when her fine brows rose inquisitively he chuckled and shook his head. 'While I was in the park I tried to decide just when it was I fell in love with you. I realised it was when I saw you racing recklessly into the surf after Matthew. I was hooked then, and as I'd made up my mind long ago that I could live without love, I started fighting you before I even knew your name!'

Kate laid her cheek against his chest, listening to the rapid pounding of his heart. 'And I thought I'd died and gone to heaven the first time I laid eyes on you,' she confessed happily. She gazed up at him, her soft hazel eyes brimming with love. 'And that's why I kept finding excuses to get over to your place. I just couldn't stay away.' She grinned impishly. 'And you were always so annoyed.'

His grin was as happy as her own. 'No, I wasn't, but of course I pretended to be. And you must remember, my darling, I found a few excuses of my own to visit you.'

They were silent for a long time, their arms wrapped around each other as they remembered their foolishness and the heartache it had caused.

Kate was the first to break the silence. 'Gerard,' she said, leaning back to look at him, 'you said you went back to the hotel to ask me to marry you.'

He nuzzled her cheek with his lips, planting burning little kisses across her smooth skin to the soft pink lobe of her shell-like ear. 'Yes,' he agreed huskily as his hands began an urgent exploration of her body.

'Well, you haven't actually asked me,' she reminded him breathlessly as he pulled her close to him.

He gazed tenderly into her eyes. 'Kate, my own sweet Kate, will you make me the happiest man on earth and become my wife?'

She didn't keep him waiting for the answer. The words were barely out of his mouth before she agreed.

'Oh, yes, my darling. How I've longed to hear those words!' She wrapped her arms around his neck and he covered her mouth with his.

The moon was high in the sky surrounded by billions of twinkling stars when they took note of their surroundings again. Their eyes were glowing and they wore the flush of passion on their cheeks.

'Goodness!' Kate exclaimed. 'The real estate agent!'

'He came before you arrived,' Gerard drawled mysteriously, one arm draped possessively across her shoulders.

'He did?'

'Yup.'

'And you spoke to him?'

'I did.'

'What did you say?'

'I told him I wanted to buy the place and he told me what it was worth. I agreed and signed the contract and a copy is on its way to your father. As soon as he signs, then the place becomes ours!' His arm tightened around her as he bent his head to kiss her. 'What do you think of that!'

Her eyes were brimming with joy. 'I . . . I think that's just . . . wonderful!' She looked teasingly up at him, her eyes sparkling. 'I always thought you secretly loved this place.'

'It's enough that you do,' he said, smiling down at her upturned face. 'When Matthew came running in to tell me there was a man tramping all over Kate's garden, I saw red! I couldn't get over here fast enough.'

Kate chuckled. 'Oh dear, I hope you didn't frighten the poor fellow!'

'I think I must have. He was very happy to leave!' Gerard slipped his arms around her slender waist. 'I love you so much, Kate darling, that it terrifies me to think I almost lost you.' His eyes darkened. 'Was I so very cruel to you?'

'You were harder on yourself,' she said with her usual honesty, and snuggled against him. 'What if I hadn't driven up for Christmas?'

'You said you would.'

'But what if I hadn't,' Kate teased. 'Would I have lost out on your proposal?'

His eyes gleamed down at her. 'Not a chance! And I'll tell you something else,' he growled. 'I wouldn't have taken no for an answer!' He kissed her hard, leaving her breathless. 'But I wanted to propose here instead of Brisbane,' he said, leading her on to the front porch. Under the moonlight, silvery sands gave way to foam-charged surf while stars danced daintily across heaven's velvet carpet. This was their Bargara, their beautiful Bargara by the sea.

He took her hand. 'Shall we go and tell Matthew?'

The stars were reflected in her eyes when she answered joyfully, 'Yes!'

When Matthew was told that his daddy was going to marry Kate he had but one urgent question. 'Does that mean you're going to be my *mummy*?'

'That's what it means, old son,' Kate assured him, ruffling his hair and hugging him. When she released him he did a series of cartwheels across the room. It was a fitting response. Kate knew it was his way of welcoming her into the family.

When Mrs Abbott was told, Kate thought she would be surprised, but she wasn't. 'I've been waiting for this to happen ever since Gerard called you "a little hothead!" ' She looked smilingly at Gerard. 'Do you think you'll be able to tame her?'

Gerard chuckled and ran his hand lovingly through Kate's copper-coloured curls. 'Why tamper with perfection?' he said as she raised her eyes to meet his, their absorption in each other complete, their love shining from their eyes.

Mrs Abbott wisely left the room, but Matthew remained. He stood looking at his father and Kate for a long time. He liked the way they were kissing each other. It made him feel all warm and happy inside. He wanted to jump and shout and do all sorts of crazy things, but most of all he wanted to tell them how much he loved them.

Kate and Gerard turned to him and they saw how happy he was feeling. They knelt and stretched out their arms and Matthew raced into them. Their arms closed around him in a tender circle of love. He tried to say how much he loved them, but there was this big lump in his throat and he found he couldn't utter a single word.

To his amazement he saw that his daddy and Kate had tears in their eyes and that they couldn't speak either. The tears didn't worry him, they were happy tears, not sad tears at all. When he felt their arms tightening around him he hugged them back with all his might and he knew this was enough!

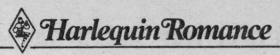
❖ Harlequin Romance

Coming Next Month

Available in May wherever paperback books are sold, or
through Harlequin Reader Service.

In the U.S.   In Canada
901 Fuhrmann Blvd.   P.O. Box 603
P.O. Box 1397   Fort Erie, Ontario
Buffalo, N.Y. 14240-1397   L2A 5X3

PATRICIA MATTHEWS

America's First Lady of Romance upholds her long
standing reputation as a bestselling romance novelist
with . . .

Enchanted

Caught in the steamy heat of America's New South,
Rebecca Trenton finds herself torn between two
brothers—she yearns for one but a dark secret binds
her to the other.

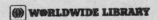

What the press says about Harlequin romance fiction...

"When it comes to romantic novels... Harlequin is the indisputable king."
—*New York Times*

"...always with an upbeat, happy ending."
—*San Francisco Chronicle*

"Women have come to trust these stories about contemporary people, set in exciting foreign places."
—*Best Sellers*, New York

"The most popular reading matter of American women today."
—*Detroit News*

"...a work of art."
—*Globe & Mail*, Toronto

Take 4 novels and a surprise gift FREE

New This spring

Harlequin Category Romance Specials!

New Mix

4 Regencies—for more wit, tradition, etiquette . . . and romance

2 Gothics—for more suspense, drama, adventure . . . and romance

Regencies

A Hint of Scandal by Alberta Sinclair
She was forced to accept his offer of marriage, but could she live with her decision?

The Primrose Path by Jean Reece
She was determined to ruin his reputation and came close to destroying her own!

Dame Fortune's Fancy by Phyllis Taylor Pianka
She knew her dream of love could not survive the barrier of his family tradition. . . .

The Winter Picnic by Dixie McKeone
All the signs indicated they were a mismatched couple, yet she could not ignore her heart's request. . . .

Gothics

Mirage on the Amazon by Mary Kistler
Her sense of foreboding did not prepare her for what lay in waiting at journey's end. . . .

Island of Mystery by Margaret M. Scariano
It was the perfect summer job, or so she thought—until it became a nightmare of danger and intrigue.

Don't miss any of them!

BPA-CAT87-1